a fantasy anthology

INTO
THE
WOODS

featuring stories by

Ross M. Kitson

Shaun Allan

Stephen Swartz 🍁 Connie J. Jasperson 🍁 Marilyn Rucker
Carlie M. A. Cullen 🍁 Lee French 🍁 Lisa Zhang Wharton
Alison DeLuca 🍁 Irene Roth Luvaul

Graphics © Lee French
Front Cover-- Golden Temple 2 © Unholyvault | Dreamstime.com
Back Cover—Magic Lamps In The Fairytale Wood © Assnezana | Dreamstime.com

Special thanks to Myrddin Editors
Connie J. Jasperson
Irene Roth Luvaul
Alison Deluca

Published by
Myrddin Publishing Group
Contact us at - www.myrddinpublishing.com

Myrddin Publishing

unique electronic & print books

:

This book would not exist without the tireless efforts of Lee French, Alison Deluca, Connie Jasperson, and Irene Roth Luvaul. And of course, the wonderful Myrddin authors whose works are represented in these pages!

Into the Woods: an anthology

TABLE OF CONTENTS

One day I happened across a wonderful image of a house in a forest. Of course, the image was copyrighted and was not available for this volume, but I was inspired—what if I offered my fellow Myrddin authors a selection of similar images? What sort of works would they come up with?

What followed was an amazing selection of short stories—some horror, some romance—but all of them fantasy and all of it wonderful. I hope you enjoy this collection of short stories as much as I do!

Connie J. Jasperson
November 2015

A PECULIAR SYMBIOSIS
By Alison DeLuca

Robert walks into the room, tosses his wallet on the dresser, and starts to unbutton his shirt. On the bed, Emily rolls over, blinks, and watches him with her usual straight gaze. "Not good," he replies to her unspoken question. "I don't know why I went."

She pats the space on the bed beside her. It's an invitation to remove his stiff denim and mismatched socks. Robert undresses quickly, throws his clothes on the wide pine slats of the bedroom floor, and avoids her eye. "Get them in the morning," he mutters.

The sheets are cool underneath his back, skin sticky from the summer air outside and the bus ride back from the city. Robert eyes Emily's generous hips under the covers and wishes he could reach out, touch the creamy skin. "She didn't know who Jerry Garcia was," he admits. The date was set up by a friend who promised a good time with dancing and drinks. Robert scratches his chest, trying to erase the feeling of plastic seats and the smell of the bus, a peculiar blend of urinals and bacon. "Jerry Garcia. I mean, I could see maybe, maybe, Phil Lesh or Bob Weir. But *Jerry Garcia,* Em!"

He picks up the clunky TV remote, and Emily's cheeks compress so two tiny dimples pop beside her lips. Robert turns on the television set and lowers the volume so it's a background hum in the darkened bedroom. Their house lies so far into the woods they only receive one channel. It's a 24-hour round of old educational movies: grainy films of girls learning about menstruation and drug warnings aimed at teens wearing loafers and knee socks. Robert reaches out his left hand. She slowly uncurls her elbow and allows her palm to hover over his – the closest they can come to touch.

On the tiny set, Bud and Jack want to go into the liquor store and buy a pint of whiskey. Robert has seen enough Coronet Films to know where the story's going. The athlete has to be a "sport," has to drink enough to feel "tight." The narrator moves to scientific explanations about frontal lobes, helped along by an amateurish sketch of a man with a cliff-like chin, displaying an exposed brain. At the end one of the teens is killed in an accident before blocky letters on tooled vinyl thank the Inglewood Police Department for their cooperation in making the film.

Robert turns off the television and throws the remote on the oval rug by the bed. He lies on his side, facing Emily. She turns and mirrors his position, one leg bent up so their knees nearly brush. Robert wonders what happened to those actors in the film. Did Bud and Jack ever break out of Inglewood? Was anyone a success or make it in the movies? Did Bud ever play King Lear? Or did they become Fuller Brush salesmen, dependent on bought women and whiskey in real life?

Morning increases the illusion of life in a treehouse. Even the rooms downstairs are green and alive, the windows filled with the ceaseless motion of leaves. Robert brews coffee, pours a cup, and heads onto the porch of the house, originally built for Russian loggers in the 1920's.

Emily already sits on the top step, still in her long sleepshirt. She leans back against a column support and tilts her head up to watch him. A ray of sunlight exposed by the tossing branches hits her forehead, making her squint. Her expression, as always, is calm.

Already soothed after the disastrous date of the night before, Robert sits next to her and sips. The brew scalds his palate.

Indoors, their old rotary phone jangles into life. Robert doesn't move. Emily fixes him with her stare, and he puts down his cup. "What?" he asks. "They'll hang up eventually." Emily doesn't move. "Oh, all right," Robert snaps.

He flounders into the house. Already blinded by the rays of sunshine, Robert feels for the phone and nearly knocks it off Emily's pine tallboy. As soon as he picks up the receiver, he hears Willa's sigh. "So I have to get your signature on a bunch of papers," she says, launching straight into her directive without bothering to say hello.

"A bunch of papers about what?"

"How should I know? Something Mom did for the school years ago. And it gets worse. We both have to sign and get it notarized."

Robert feels a frosty hand grip his guts. It's not that he doesn't love his daughter, but he's already bracing for the inevitable argument they always have. He knows no one can be the dad spouting advice in the "Am I Trustworthy?" film he watched with Emily a few nights ago, realizes that the ideal father doesn't exist nor ever existed. Still, he wants to be able to reach through the wall of spikes Willa has put up around herself ever since – well. Ever since February.

"We can use our bank," he offers. He can't go into town again on the bus that smells like bad bacon. He simply cannot do it.

"I got my notary's license a few weeks ago. I'll be there tonight." There's a click followed by a hollow dial tone.

Robert wanders back onto the porch. The air is warm on his forearms, exposed as he rolls up the sleeves of his pajama shirt. His skin, always darker than Emily's smooth, sandy brown, has faded lately, become ashy. Probably he needs to get outside more.

"Willa's coming for a visit," he tells his wife. Her face creases with a smile.

Emily stands up and heads into the thick trees, not waiting to see if he'll follow. Of course he does. Her squat figure negotiates bushes and pooled rain among sodden leaves. He's the one who gets stuck to a creeping thistle and has to detach one pant leg from the stickers.

She stops and holds up one plump arm. Robert moves forward and sees a tiny patch of ground roped off with a complex system of cane and looped string to keep away deer. Inside are clumps of blackberry bushes already dotted with fruit. It's a secret garden, a tiny treasure just for him. "Are these Willa's berries?" he asks, and Emily nods. She walks right through the string and cane fence to move between the canes of clustered fruit.

Carefully Robert climbs into the space. His pants snag again on the fence and the sharp claws of the blackberries. He doesn't have a bucket or even an old Tupperware container, but he strips off his pajama shirt and ties it into a clumsy bag. Emily watches as he picks berries, shaking her head when he goes for the ones that aren't the color of a fresh bruise. Some are still white, waiting stubbornly for time and sun to bring them to life.

He's forgotten about the flies. By the time he's picked a few handfuls, his chest is striped with purple marks where he's slapped away the no-see-ems. "Guess it's time to go back," he mutters. But when he turns he's already alone, trapped inside the cane and prickly ropes of fruit.

On the way back to the house, he gets lost twice. Robert has never been one for direction. When they drove Willa to Avon for a rare day at the beach, Emily always had to tell him where to turn. He hasn't dared to drive anywhere since February. Instead he has to take the bus.

Robert really hates the bus.

Several times he feels panic nearly throttle him. Woods can cause irrational fear – he read it somewhere. The police chief of Inglewood wouldn't be afraid among the trees, though. The man would take out his compass, line it up with the sun, and divine the way home for him and the lost children who had foolishly wandered off alone.

It's a real movie, right? Robert is certain he's seen it before on the 24-hour channel.

The sight of Emily through the trees sends a spear of relief through him. Her face is flat with the silly little nose he used to grab between his knuckles. Robert knows her features, the curve of her cheekbones, and the way her chin cupped into his palm, better than anything, even better than his tall, gangly body.

Emily leads the way back to their house. It's cooler inside, and Robert feels the hair on his arms stand up. He has to stoop slightly to enter the kitchen where an index card sits by the stove. The edges are browned with age, and a recipe is written out in Emily's untidy writing: *Willa's Blackberry Buckle.*

"Mom set it up a year ago and didn't tell anyone." Willa sits at the table across from Robert. The papers she's brought fan across the beaded tablemats Emily bought at a Dead concert years ago. A group of rainbow bears march across the mats and grin at Robert. He doesn't feel like smiling back.

"What is it again?"

He watches her struggle to repress a long sigh. "I already told you. Mom set up a trust fund for the college to fund organic research – hydroponics, local produce, the whole bit." Willa stabs one of the papers on the table. "Didn't you know about any of this while she was doing it?"

Robert doesn't answer. It's quite possible Emily told him and he was in one of his funks, planning their next concert trip. He gets up and fetches the foil-covered pan, brings it to the table and removes the cover.

Willa's brow crinkles up like a potato chip. "Is it Mom's – don't tell me you made Blackberry Buckle."

"Found the recipe." Now he's uncovered the cake, Robert realizes the smell is reminiscent of Emily. The butter, eggs, and berries combine to bring her back in the kitchen, her broad back bent over the oven.

4

"Oh, my God." Willa slumps over her forearms, careless of the papers. Her shoulders shake. Robert wonders if he should get up again, put a hand on her neck. His daughter's skin seems defenseless, so smooth and dusted with tiny curls. Just below the hairline, she has a tiny mark of vitiligo. Robert hasn't seen it since Willa sobbed in Emily's arms over a forgotten childhood tragedy decades ago.

He can't summon the energy to get out of his chair. Instead he cuts a piece of the buckle, puts it on a paper plate, and hands it to Willa. When she looks up, her eyelids are rimmed red, a messy geisha. She blows her nose into a napkin but doesn't eat the cake. "I thought I'd never see it again after February…"

The statement propels Robert to his feet. "Don't talk about February."

"Jesus, Dad. You're worse than I thought. We have to confront…"

Robert walks away to the sink and turns on both taps as high as they'll go. The sound of water covers his daughter's voice, and the tap runs and runs until the steam blotches the window behind Emily's plants still in their rooting jars. The slips of parsley and cilantro have grown so much the roots are starting to come out the sides.

"Dad." Willa is next to him. "You won't even look at me. Not once since it happens."

He swipes a hand over his face. Willa has Emily's flat nose and firm chin. He doesn't want to share those things with anyone else.

Through the window, he sees Emily hiding behind one of the trees near the house. Dimples bracket her full mouth. With any other woman, it would mean amusement, but when Emily dimples, it's a sign of annoyance.

He returns to the table and sits in the chair so old the legs wobble when he leans over the papers. "What do I need to do?"

"First, you need to understand this shifts half of what Mom left you to the college. It'll eat into your annuity."

Robert picks up the pen. "I don't care. Don't spend anything anyway." He can eat the buckle for a few days. Food tastes like cotton wool lately, in any case, and he certainly doesn't plan on any more dates. Emily has jars of flaxseed in the freezer, and there's plenty of flour left after baking. He'll ask her about the beer bread recipe card next.

He signs next to Willa's finger, taken aback by how shaky his handwriting looks on the line. When he finishes, Willa holds a fork, and firmly she waves it in front of his mouth. "Eat something," she insists.

Her dimples pop out – another item she inherited from her mother. Robert bites into the cake just so he has an excuse to close his eyes. When he opens them again, the dimples are gone.

Willa makes him walk her to the car parked outside. "The road is terrible," she says.

"So you say each time you come over." He can't wait to get back inside and find Emily.

She ducks her head to put the folder of college papers on the passenger seat and gets into the car. "Sure you're okay with this? Last chance to back out. We could fight the will, say it was done under duress or something."

"Are *you* okay with it?" It's her money too, after all, or at least it will be one day.

"Yeah, I think it's great. Going to be an amazing department – she was ahead of her time. But I worry about you all alone among the pines."

But I'm not alone. He says nothing, watches her start the car and pull out onto the sanded lane. When she slaps the car door as a final goodbye, Robert realizes Willa has driven off and he won't see her again for weeks. Months, maybe.

The little slap, her arm crooked like a flesh staple, makes his head buzz with an unreachable memory. He's seen it before, maybe in one of the Inglewood movies. It's an old-fashioned signal used by cruisers to start races or fights.

Robert returns to the house and wanders into the kitchen to open the refrigerator. The shelves are empty aside from the bowl of leftover blackberries. He could walk to the nearest Wawa and buy milk, except it would mean leaving the house. And didn't Emily leave powdered soya in the cupboards? It'll be fine.

When he closes the door and sees Emily planted next to him, sturdy on her thickened legs and round knees, Robert heaves a vast sigh. Relief burns through his gut like day-old coffee, and he thinks he could do without milk, without the berries in the chipped bowl, even without Willa as long as his wife stays in the house. "You little minx," he breathes to cover the excited roar of blood in his ears. "Set up the college department on the sly, did you? While I slept, or in the middle of one of those dumb movies?"

She smiles and doesn't respond: an irresistible mystery.

After Willa's visit, the days flit by in a firefly spiral. July arrives with the usual spate of heat waves, but under the canopy of pines, the atmosphere is shadowy, cool, hushed. Robert wakes each morning on his side facing his wife, but he never catches her asleep. Emily's eyes, slanted down at the corners, are always open. Black pupils fix on his, and when he stretches out his hand, she covers it with hers. It's the most intimate act he's ever experienced, creating a flight of sparks in his belly so explosive he pants for breath.

How long have they been married? Twenty-five years since they met at the Dead concert, introduced by Emily's college roommate. Fay, he thinks her name was. Fay told them they seemed like harmonic souls, and he longed to prove her wrong. But Emily's straight gaze and bushy hair captured his interest right away, and after hours of dancing and fragrant smoke, he woke up in her camper bed. Ten weeks later she called him with the news that she was pregnant.

Twenty-five years. Over two decades. The day Emily received her MA and got her first job at the local college – the same one about to benefit from the bulk of her money. A blur of raising a baby he never planned, fixing up her little house, teaching her to drive. Being annoyed when she forgot his tea. Spending entire days without saying a word to each other. She was part of the furniture, and so, Robert supposes, was he.

It all ends in February, a time he skips over in his mind. The red swiped across the road, the motionless arm sticking out from under an orange tarp. February is a month he can carve out of his calendar, cutting up time as though it were a melon.

Emily's hand moves over his wrist, up his inner arm to cover Robert's shoulder. He holds his breath in the boat of their little bed. Just as he once did in eighth grade when he asked out Ruby Jackson, Robert tries and discards several mental conversations. *Do you like this?* he wants to ask his wife. *Shall we go and see if there are more blackberries?*

And, most important of all, *Will you stay?*

It's the happiest summer he's ever experienced, even if he can't feel Emily's touch on palm or shoulder. Perhaps touch doesn't matter when you're falling in love. Perhaps it's enough to watch her stumpy little body lead through the trees to the blackberry patch with its canes bowed under sweet fruit.

Robert ignores what he calls the cold pricklies on his spine. They come in quick little rushes, acid baths of "what next." And... *something* has happened to the Inglewood movies when he watches television at night. When he can't sleep.

Except he doesn't want to think about television any longer.

Instead, Robert gets up early, makes pancakes with the last of the flour, eats them with blackberries and hot water on the porch. The coffee is gone, but he can't bear the thought of leaving the little house to go and buy more. Didn't he read somewhere you could make tea from blackberry leaves?

The next time Emily leads him to the hidden patch in the woods, Robert picks a bag of those leaves and brings them back to their kitchen. He soaks them in hot water, tastes the bitter brew, and throws it away out of the window. The liquid arcs in a green wave, sparkling under the spears of sunlight through the thick pines.

Because the Inglewood movies *have* changed. Robert tries to sleep early, but he wakes up at three in the morning to stare at the tiny TV, unaccountably turned on in their bedroom. Emily lies on her side to watch him as his mouth droops with horror from what he sees on the screen. When he makes himself get out of bed to shut off the television with a shudder no less violent than the reaction to blackberry-leaf tea, she allows him to hover his palm over hers.

Robert floats back to sleep eventually, and in the morning he moves the television to the pile of stuff in the basement. His eyes squinch so he can't see the shoes, the sweaters, her winter coat, Emily's dresses piled up in old drawstring bags she used to take to the beach.

His heart pounds from the climb back to the kitchen from the dark cellar. Emily stands at the sink, smooth face looking out into the pine needles. Robert goes behind her, props one arm on each side of her wide, generous hips. The rocket in his chest booms as she tilts her head just right to smile at him.

There's a can of artichoke hearts he's been saving in the pantry. Robert dusts it off with his sleeve, opens the can, and pours the gray contents into one of Emily's hummingbird bowls. He eats one, but the mush is so salty his mouth puckers. The rest of the can follow the tea into the woods. Blackberries, sharp and seed-crunchy under his teeth, chase away the metallic taste of canned food.

The phone rings, and Emily steps firmly out of sight. Robert's heart sinks as she disappears into the little sitting room filled with shadows. Reluctantly he goes to the phone and picks up the receiver.

"Dad?" It's Willa's voice, loud with annoyance. "Dad, for chrissake say hello. Do I need to send the EMTs?"

Robert says hello to keep his little world safe. "What do you want?"

"The transfer went through. Sayreville Community College invited us to a reception. They're naming the department after Mom." Her words get blurred, and with a shock, Robert hears Willa crying on the other end of the phone.

"Willa," he says, one hand hanging loose by the corduroy shorts Emily always made fun of whenever he wore them. The patch over his left knee is stained with purple juice. "I guess I don't know what to say."

"Nothing new there." Her quick intake of breath is followed by a prolonged nose-blow. "So will you come with me?"

"Come where?"

"I just said. The reception Sayreville's throwing for us. Be my date? It'd be nice. Just you and me. We can talk, yeah? We haven't really been able to sit down since…"

"Blue jay just flew into the window. Gotta go." Anything to head off the words she's about to say.

Robert crashes the receiver into the cradle. When he turns, Emily's in the doorway, one dimple dark against the swell of her cheek.

"You asked me to the dance, for crying out loud!"

"Watch your language, Timmy. I don't appreciate fresh boys."

Robert sits up. The television is back in the bedroom. Who moved it in? And when?

An old Valentine's Day dance flickers on the set where a blond bobbysoxer with pin curls argues with her hulk of a date. Behind them the small, thin, rejected boy watches from the shadows, ready to go and defend the blonde's honor.

The picture is wrong. None of the actors have faces. Timmy's head is blank as an egg beneath the widow's peak of his crew cut.

In the crumpled sheets, Robert can't move. He knows Timmy and his blond date wait outside the bedroom door. Any movement or attempt to escape will bring the cast of "The Shy Guy" pouring into the room, arms outstretched to feel for warm flesh. Since they don't have eyes, they have to walk like that, he tells himself.

He shakes his head at the nonsense in his brain. Emily moves closer and holds up her palm for him to touch, but Robert huffs and flops back on the bed. It's not enough any longer. He wants to roll her back into the pillows, to mouth the soft skin over her neck, map the sweet pouch of her belly, to thrust inside her warmth. Those things have been stolen from him, and he'd cut off his arm to have them again.

On the screen, Timmy tries whispering into the blond girl's ear. The Shy Guy frowns, puffs up his lips in exaggerated frustration, and removes a knife from his pocket.

Robert sits up and scoots to the end of the bed. This isn't how it's supposed to go in Inglewood. His breath rattles as Shy Guy gets Timmy's elbow and, with one quick motion, slices off the larger boy's arm. The black and white footage makes the explosion look black, but Robert knows it's red, just like the blond girl's lipstick and the cut-out hearts decorating the gym wall.

"Aw, gee, whacha go and do that for?" Timmy's voice is a screech of pain.

He tries not to listen as he feels for the remote. The slippery plastic lies under the bed, and Robert turns off the television with his eyes closed tight shut so he won't see any more. The bed creaks under his body as he gets under warm sheets (washed only with hot water since they've run out of detergent), and he wishes he could shrimp his body around the bulk of Emily's hips.

When he gets dressed in the morning, none of his pants fit. They hang loosely over his hips, pooch at the back. *Maybe it's okay,* Robert thinks. Perhaps this is the way it should be – he'll whittle himself down to nothing until he can dig himself into a slot under the earth and touch his wife again.

The thought is so dark he hums to hide it, but Emily has already caught his guilty, sidelong look in the mirror. He sees her reflection behind his, telltale dimples popped out and firm arms folded over her chest.

For breakfast, Robert finds a few hamburger buns in the back of the freezer and manages to hack the bag out with a screwdriver from the junk drawer. Even toasted, the buns are hard and white on the edges from freezer burn.

Grocery shopping means the bus ride, other people, conversation or at least an exchange of words. No, he can't possibly go through such a weary, boring process.

So when the phone rings, Robert rushes out of the room onto the porch, grabs a bucket, and flaps off to the berry patch. He's nearly pantsed by a stray branch on the way back to the house, bucket echoing with the last of the fruit.

"What is menstruation like? Well, Debbie-Sue, it feels like this." The nurse brings her fist down and rams a screwdriver into the girl's stomach. Black blood sprays over Debbie-Sue's face, and the tool quivers in torn abdominal muscle. *"Don't be a little baby,"* the nurse says. *"Everyone has to go through the onset of the Curse."*

Robert shudders and turns off the television. Who turned it on in the first place? He sits on the side of the bed and lets his wrists hang over spread thighs. A white column resolves in front of him. Thank goodness it's Emily, wearing his old t-shirt—her usual version of a nightgown. When Robert holds out his palm, she shakes her head and walks backward from the bed.

Just like the original trip to the berry patch, Robert gets the idea he's supposed to follow. Useless words stick in his throat: *No. Stop. Emily. Not yet.*

Outside the trees mask moon and stars, but when they reach the sanded road, heavenly light illuminates Emily's upright back and smooth calves revealed by the long hem of the old t-shirt. He bought it at a Dead concert, and she stole it from him since it was big enough to cover her pregnancy. Now the letters are obscured by multiple washings, a worn gravestone for a tour long gone.

Although he suspects what is about to happen, Robert's chest seizes when they turn a corner to see the bus waiting under a yellow lamp. Emily walks forward, never hesitating until her hand is on the vehicle's bent rail. There she stops and turns to face him where he has frozen beside a clump of Jack-in-the-Pulpit plants and a greasy bag of White Castle, discarded by shoobees on the way home from the beach.

Even now he wants to run, catch the tail of the faded t-shirt, and push her back into the pines lining the wood road. God, the feeling of her lips under his, his tongue in her mouth. He would have her on the soft pine needles in full view of everyone in the bus.

But the doors close with a steamy hiss, and an ancient engine whines with protest. The stately behind of the old bus flickers in and out with the yellow light until it disappears altogether.

Does she open the window and put out her arm to slap the side as a final goodbye? Robert's eyes stream with water. It's impossible to see the final glimpse.

The 24-hour channel no longer shows the Inglewood movies. There is nothing left but static.

THE FOREST HOUSE
By Connie J. Jasperson

The path Janet had taken on the spur of the moment was unmarked, just a little trail leading off the graveled walking path, and she nearly missed it. It wound through a pleasant, sun-dappled wood, filled with the clean scents of cedar and fir, reminding her of the forests of her childhood home.

She enjoyed the relief from the heat of a September afternoon and wandered along. The sounds of a woodpecker and the low hoo-hoo-hoo of mourning doves, accented with the occasional warbler's song to soothe her, eased her homesickness. She tied her cardigan about her waist by its sleeves, wondering how long summer would hang on before the rains of autumn set in.

She'd only been a resident of Littleton for one month, but she liked it. The small university town was easily walkable, well-known for its many hiking trails. That was fine by her as she didn't own a car. Janet was not without means, but she was careful with her money. She had her stipend from the university and her job as teaching assistant while she finished her graduate studies, and she liked her job.

That morning she had dressed as she always did for a warm day, in a long, gauzy skirt and light blouse, with a sweater to keep her warm in the chill of the morning. She left her rooms wearing hiking sandals with no stockings, as the dog-days of summer had set in in Littleton, and afternoons could be unbearably warm.

Not realizing how deep inside the forest she was, Janet walked under a canopy that was only beginning to turn colors, feeling the stress leave her. Finally free to just think, she considered her advisor and how her research was progressing. She was three weeks into the school year, and she was still unsure of what to make of the professor who was her advisor.

She had been assured that Professor Thomlinsen was the only professor who could assist her in her area of study, but she was having trouble forging any kind of mental connection with him. There was nothing memorable about him, although he was pleasant enough. Clean-shaven, with his drab, blondish hair pulled back in the obligatory professorial ponytail, he appeared young for a man of his credentials. His slight Danish accent was barely noticeable, and he had been educated at the great universities in Europe. Knowing that, she was slightly intimidated and thought he must be older than he looked.

She had no complaints about him as an advisor, but he was distant, hard to read. She thought of him often but didn't know why. Blue eyes, set above high cheekbones—he had all the components of a handsome man, but something was lacking. Even so, she was once again thinking of him as a man, and not as her advisor.

It was just...when he discussed the possible origins of the many folk ballads collected by Francis Child, he became animated, inspired by his obsession. Despite that, Professor Thomlinsen didn't have the cult following of undergrad females that many in his position might have, so perhaps only she felt that fleeting charm.

She sighed. It occurred to her that she was no different from the professor—she too was a pale reflection of the students around her, unstylish, slightly out of step, and living in the lore and books of the past. It was Friday, and she had no plans other than walking the long way home and then studying all night, while other women her age were meeting their boyfriends and heading out to nightclubs. Plowing her way through old manuscripts written in Middle English had never allowed her much time for partying, or a social life in general.

Her stomach grumbled, and Janet nearly tripped on a heavy root. She realized she had been walking far longer than she had intended, and now the chill of late evening penetrated her awareness. She drew her cardigan more closely around her, buttoning it.

She wished she'd thought to pack a granola bar. She sipped the last of her water and pulled out her phone to check the time. It had apparently gone dead, although she remembered it had a good charge when she checked the time earlier that afternoon. *I've grown too dependent on these things*, she thought. Frustration surged, and stuffing it down, she turned to walk back the way she had come.

The trail was gone.

No matter where she looked, she couldn't see her path home. The only way she could see led deeper into the forest, beginning at the spot where she stood. Confused, she turned again. She stood in a small clearing, and now she saw that she'd apparently come down a long, steep hill into a valley. That seemed odd because she hadn't noticed her descent as she walked, but now tall, forested hills rose all around her, the golden larches on the highest peaks reflecting the last rays of the setting sun. Her breath caught at the sight. "So beautiful. The larches—they shine like a beacon."

The sun set, and the glorious vision faded. In the gathering gloom, she looked around her. Surely she hadn't become lost. The trail had seemed well defined, easy to follow. In fact, she'd been able to walk it with no effort at all, her mind on other things than where she set her feet. Perhaps the growing twilight disguised the trail. Shadows had deepened all around her and it was difficult to see very far.

Once again, Janet turned to look in front of her. Ahead, the trail flattened out, faint, but clear even in the dusk of early evening. This deep in the forest, autumn had arrived in full force with red and gold leaves drifting down, slowly wafting to the forest floor.

She decided she must have strayed from her original path and began walking forward, hoping the track would lead her back to the part of town she was familiar with. Not wanting to be in the forest after nightfall, her steps quickened until she became breathless and had to slow her progress down the path.

Regardless of her efforts, she was still deep in the woods when complete darkness fell. In the dark, she could see the path as it wound through the eerie, shadowed forest. A prickling sensation sent shivers through her, the feeling of being observed by unfriendly eyes, and again she began hurrying, almost panicking.

Her backpack had grown heavy, the weight of her laptop and textbooks dragging on her shoulders. The night was chill, with a hint of frost in the air despite it being only late September. A wind sprang up, biting and cold. Reluctantly, Janet stopped to pull her hoodie out of her backpack, putting on it over her sweater, which helped some, but her hands and cheeks were quite cold, as were her legs.

Her fingers were thick and fumbling, but she managed to zip it and pulled the sleeves down over her hands. She drew the hood over her head, and immediately her ears felt better. The chill still permeated, but at least the hoodie blocked some of the breeze that rattled limbs and blew leaves across her path.

Feeling the pressure of unseen eyes, she hurried forward, as she had no choice. As she walked, the forest grew shadowy and eerie, but beneath the scattering of dead, dry leaves, the silvery path was clearly visible through the darkness.

At last, to her intense relief, she seemed to be approaching the town again. Through the trees, a warm light glimmered in the window of a house, and the scent of a wood fire seemed to linger in the cool night air. As she neared it, she realized to her disappointment that the house stood alone in a small clearing, completely surrounded by the dark, dense forest. No other lights shone through the trees.

Now, with a sinking heart, she realized that somehow she had inadvertently left the town of Littleton and gone into the wild. How far she had come or where she was in relation to town, she had no idea, but clearly she was miles away from home.

She had left the university at two-thirty. Her empty stomach and the utter darkness told her she had been walking at least five or six hours. At that rate she could be anywhere, but surely the people in that house would offer her some directions and perhaps allow her to use their telephone.

As Janet approached the house in the clearing, she could see in the moonlight a rose-covered stone cottage, with round windows and a thatched roof. A vegetable garden surrounded by a withy fence still contained some late crops, pumpkins and such.

But the house was what really drew her eye. Even in the gray of moonlight, it was amazing, an illustration from a book of fairytales. *How strange,* she thought, *to find such whimsy in the heart of nowhere.* The house had a magical quality, reminding her of why she sought out and studied old ballads and fairytales so intensely.

Gathering her courage, she lifted the heavy iron knocker and brought it down on the ornately-carved, wooden door.

The door swung open under the pressure of her knock, revealing a large, candle-lit room. Janet entered and the door closed behind her. A fire blazed in the fireplace, and she was irresistibly drawn to it, walking past a large, rough wooden table, flanked by two benches. Her footsteps were muffled as she crossed the bare stone floor. Her body shivered as she soaked up the heat.

A slight sound caught her attention, and her eyes were drawn to a doorway, where a stunningly handsome man stood framed, watching her. She jumped, flushing. "Oh! Please, forgive me for invading your home without your permission. The door just opened, and I found myself entering." Her excuse sounded weak, even to her.

He crossed the room, welcoming her with a smile. "If the door opened for you, then you're meant to be here." He seemed very familiar, but she couldn't place him. He was a man she would never have forgotten. His dark eyes were intense and alive, and his golden hair curled around his shoulders, shining in the firelight. His unconscious charm was overwhelming, and she was nearly stricken dumb. No one, not even a movie star, ever had that kind of impact on her.

"I'll put your possessions here." He set her backpack on bench beside the door and hung her hoodie on a hook above it, where it looked small and odd beside his brown cloak.

Then, taking her arm, he seated her at the table on the bench nearest the fire.

Numbly, she wondered what would happen next.

"I'm Tam. I rarely have company, so please, forgive my manners, letting you stand there so long." His speech was slightly accented, in a way she couldn't quite identify, but which sounded rather Danish, like Professor Thomlinsen. In fact, Tam reminded her very much of her professor, only alive and real in way most people never were.

From somewhere far away, she dredged up her manners. "Oh, no. I should be apologizing to you. I'm Janet."

"I know." He nodded, confusing her. "Let me get you something warm to drink and perhaps some soup. You look famished."

Feeling completely out of her depth, she tried to get her balance back, choosing to assume he understood she was embarrassed. "You're being too kind. But, yes, I am hungry, starving, really."

His smile lit his face, and he left the room, going to his kitchen, she presumed. She sat, warming by the fire, but stunned, robbed of her ability to think.

He returned bearing a tray holding a simple meal for two: thick slices of warm, dark bread and honey to spread on it and two bowls filled with a delicious smelling vegetable soup. Suddenly, Janet was ravenous, but she waited as he set them before her and went back into the kitchen. Almost immediately he returned again with a pot of tea and two mugs. She sipped it, finding it an herbal tea with hints of apple.

Seating himself opposite her, he gestured to the food. "Please, eat. You've walked far today and taken a chill. You need to get warmed." He spread honey on a slice of bread and handed it to her. His hesitant smile took her breath away, but she managed to take the bread without dropping it. She savored the sweet taste, feeling as if she had never before eaten anything as good and never would again.

They ate in silence, which felt award until she realized he was unused to talking. Then she didn't know how to break it. As the starved feeling left her and a sense of wellbeing grew, she took in her companion's attire. He wore clothing perfectly suited to his house: breeches gathered into knee-high boots, a shirt of white linen, laced at the throat and wrists. He was dressed as if for a renaissance fair, and perhaps he knew it. But if he did, it was clear that he didn't care. His clothes had been made well with attention to detail and historically accurate fabrics, unlike most costumes. He apparently took his chosen reality seriously.

After dinner he cleared the table. "Wait here a moment and I'll get us more tea."

Reluctantly, Janet said, "I really shouldn't prevail on your hospitality like this. I...I'm lost. I wandered off the trail, and I can't find my way back to town. If you'll be kind enough to direct me, I'll be on my way."

His eyes widened with a fleeting look of fear. "You're absolutely no trouble, and I'll gladly show you the way...but not until morning. After dark these woods are not safe for morta...people." His expression convinced her of his conviction. "I'm sorry—I have no motor vehicle."

"Bears or mountain lions?" Janet recalled the feeling of being watched and shivered. "These woods are deep. Many wild creatures must make it their home."

"Yes, wild creatures. And because they're wild, all are dangerous to humans." He looked relieved. "I've a guest room, and you're more than welcome to stay. I'll enjoy your company this evening. I've not had anyone to talk to in person for a while." His expression perplexed her, both happy and profoundly sad. "And now autumn has arrived. I knew it would come someday, but I had hoped…never mind."

The man was very confusing, cryptic. "Ah. You work from home, via the internet." She laughed. "I sometimes telecommute too."

Tam looked startled but agreed. "The internet," he said, as if the words were new. "Yes, it is convenient but solitary. I don't often leave this place." He rose from his bench. "Let me find some chairs, and we'll sit by the fire and drink mulled cider. You'll tell me all about yourself, and I will attempt to do the same."

Janet smiled. Tam's rather old-fashioned phrasings and slight accent seemed perfectly natural in that stone cottage. She watched as, from the dark corners of the room, he drew two worn but comfy wingback chairs she hadn't noticed before and set them in front of the fire, where they could watch the flames and talk. He found a wide footstool which he placed between the chairs.

"If you don't mind, we can share the footstool to warm our feet while we get to know one another." Tam's wistful smile charmed her. It was innocent and wise, and poignant in some indefinable way.

Feeling quite bold, Janet nodded. They sat before the fire, and he asked her about her work, which she was happy to talk about. "So few people are interested in the old stories."

"I know," he replied. "But they hold many mysteries if only we look closer."

The mulled cider was definitely alcoholic, but it had a soothing effect, and she forgot her anxieties as they talked about her studies. The apple aroma of the hot cider, infused with aromatic spices, filled her senses, and she sipped it carefully, not wanting to become inebriated.

He was keenly interested and quite knowledgeable about the origins of myths and legends. "But what do you think of the *Tam Lin* stories?" he finally asked, after refilling their mugs.

"I feel sure most of the tales began with a true story, perhaps one that is from far back in prehistoric times," she said. "Take the *Tam Lin* cycle. This tale is found all over Europe and Asia. There are several variations as to how Tam Lin, or Tomlin or any of the variations on his name that all are similar, found himself bespelled, and the girl's name is always Janet or Margaret or a variation on those names. Her role differs slightly from one version to the next—sometimes she bears him a love child, sometimes not, but the fact that when she agrees to help him break his curse, he is transformed into a variety of dangerous, deadly beasts in her arms remains the same. This tells me the tale began with one storyteller around one fire long, long ago, perhaps even before the Saxons came to Brittain."

He gazed into the fire, considering her words. Then, "I agree it is from long ago but not quite that far back."

It turned out he knew many variations on the tale. His intense interest in the Tam Lin stories surprised her. She assumed his interest had grown out of his name and remarked on the coincidence. He said, "It is true I am intrigued by these tales and have always been. Perhaps the name stirred my interest at first when I was very young." His voice grew soft. "Tam was the diminutive of Thomas, in the village where I was born, and thus I was known as Tam." He sounded as if he would add more, but instead he fell silent.

"My mother just liked the name Janet, and so she gave me that name. Nowadays, not too many people know about Francis Child and his life's work." She laughed. "It's too bad we don't know the actual melodies for so many of the ballads he preserved for us. He didn't write down the melodies, and many have disappeared."

Tam said, "Some of the melodies still remain, but the music isn't as important as the story. We can sing the story to any melody we choose, as long as the words are true." He gazed into the fire. "The old words spoken in the true language are what are most important."

"You remind me of my professor," she said. "He makes statements like that, but I don't know what he means."

"I know."

She cut him a sideways glance. "Why are you so enigmatic?"

Instead of answering, he asked, "Would you like to hear the true story of Tam Lin, sung to the earliest melody I know? This ballad was once very common—they often sang it in my village."

Bemused, she nodded, and disappearing into a room though a door she hadn't noticed, Tam brought out a strange musical instrument like a lute, but one more ancient in its origin, with more strings. She gasped as he began playing and singing. He was as accomplished as any trained musician she had ever heard.

> Fair Janet longs to see her love,
> Beneath the fairy moon,
> And she's away to Carterhaugh
> As fast as she can go.
>
> A babe begot by fairy man
> A child she must not bear
> Herbs will cure her of the babe
> And so weeps Janet fair
>
> Why do you pull the rose, Janet?
> Why do you break the tree?
> Why do you come to Carterhaugh
> Without the leave of me?'
>
> I must pull the rose, Tam Lin,
> The Haugh belongs to me
> I cannot bear a fairy child,
> Nor ask I leave of thee.'
>
> Full pleasant is the fairy land,
> Though mortal, there I dwell
> I'm a fairy, through Maab's spell,
> Within a mortal's shell.
>
> O pleasant is the fairy land,
> A tithe we pay to dwell
> A tithe of mortal soul we pay

I'll die this year as well.

Tomorrow morn is winter's eve,
If you should want to save my life,
To Oberon she'll send my soul
Save me from my fairy wife.

And first you'll let the black horse by,
And then let the pass the brown;
Then I'll ride on a milk-white steed,
You'll pull me to the ground.

And first, I'll grow into your arms
An asp and then an adder;
Hold me fast, let me not go,
I'll be your child's father.

Next, I'll grow into your arms
A toad and then an eel;
Hold me fast, let me not go,
If true your love for me.

Last, I'll grow into your arms
A dove and then a swan;
Then, fair Janet, let me go,
I'll be a mortal man.'

In the darkness of the room, before the fire, his voice conjured images, and Janet felt as if she lived the tale. The melody felt right, as if at last she had found the true music for the words. Tam's voice and the music of his lute consumed her, and under the spell of the music, she lost all sense of self, becoming the Janet of the tale.

She came back to herself as the music died away. "I thought I knew every version of that song."

"Even I don't know them all, though I should." Tam gazed into the fire, melancholy filling his eyes. His voice was soft when he spoke, "How odd that you are named Janet, and I am named

Tam. How odd that autumn has finally arrived, and with it a guest. It must mean something important. These things always do."

Something about his profile caught her attention. Those cheekbones…the eyes…. Suddenly Janet realized who she had spent the evening with. "Professor Thomlinsen? You're the professor…but I didn't recognize you in this place and dressed that way." Her voice rose, accusing. "What…I see you every day! You're at my school, but you said you don't get out, that you telecommute." Her intense disappointment in discovering he'd lied threatened to overwhelm her. She wanted to weep, and her words were thick as she said, "You lied to me."

He sighed. "I know it looks that way. I will have to show you something, but you can't tell anyone." His voice took on an urgency that was as compelling as it was honest. "Promise me you will tell no one."

Bemused once again, she nodded. Taking her hand, he led her into the room from where he'd gotten his lute. It was a standard medieval bedroom, with a curtained bed and a few shelves. A table stood near a window, with two chairs drawn up before it. On the table was an orb the size of a bowling ball, made entirely of quartz crystal.

Tam led her to the table and seated her. He sat opposite. "This is how I am able to telecommute." Closing his eyes, he seemed to calm and center himself. Taking a deep breath, he placed both hands on the crystal. It leapt to light, nearly blinding her, and she watched as he shimmered. Before her eyes he faded, becoming a pale, almost transparent version of himself, his features taking on the look of the Professor Thomlinsen she had come to know. Superimposed over his clothes was the attire he wore at the university.

Then, surprising her even more, he spoke, but not to her. Instead, he spoke as if to the night security guard at the university. "Good evening, Cecil. Yes, I've forgotten a folder that will be needed for my research. How's your mother doing? The surgery went well? Ah, good. Well, I won't keep you from your rounds. I will be off now. Have a good weekend."

A manila folder appeared on the table beside his elbow, and after a few moments he took his hands off the crystal. As the light in the crystal dimmed, the persona of Professor Thomlinsen faded and Tam reappeared, vivid and full of life as Professor Thomlinsen could never be. His grin was sheepish. "I have to make sure I walk away and go around a corner before I take my hands away. It frightens people when I vanish before their eyes."

Janet sat there, dumbfounded. She had so many questions but no words to ask them with, and the silence stretched.

Tam finally broke the silence. "I am tied to this house and these woods. Yes, I'm a prisoner in some ways, but this is my world. The house knew I was lonely though and wanted me to have companionship. Through the crystal I am able to be a part of the world that has passed outside my pocket of time."

Finally Janet stood up. "Let's sit by the fire again. It's cold in here." At her words, a fire leapt to life in the fireplace. She looked at him, suspicion breaking the spell his charismatic looks had had on her. "Did you do that?"

Tam shook his head. "My magic is simple fairy magic, limited now to what I can do with music. The house was created out of old magic before I was born. It has its own mind." Two mugs of mulled cider appeared by their elbows.

Janet stood and carried her mug to the main room. She stood before the fire, trying to sort out her thoughts. She went to her backpack and withdrew her laptop. Opening it, she found it dead, as if the battery had died. Suppressing a groan, she set her phone on top of it, intending to find an outlet to plug them into.

Tam stood in the doorway, holding a sheaf of paper, a quill, and a pot of ink. "This place is situated out of time. Those devices don't work. You'll have to rely on paper and pen." He set them on the table, at the place nearest the fire where she had eaten dinner. "Don't worry. When you leave, they will work just the same as they always have. And your handwritten notes should travel with you." He sat opposite her, clearly wondering what she was going to do.

She leaned her head on her hands, full of confusion and questions. Finally she looked up. "How did all this begin? And be warned, I will take notes."

He nodded. "Frank—Francis—Child said the same, although he wanted to know my father's story and was not interested in mine. This house didn't appear much different than any other

24

cottage of the day, and my story was not as intriguing as my father's."

Janet dipped the quill into the inkpot and began detailing her day to that moment, trying to be as legible as she could, although writing with a quill was a little different than writing with a modern pen. She had always used a laptop or eTablet to take notes and done very little writing other than the basic classes in elementary school, so her penmanship was poor. She struggled with the unfamiliar quill to form the letters so they could be read. A candle appeared on the table, shedding a bit more light on her work, but still the room was dark.

Leaning forward and reading her efforts upside down, Tam chuckled. "I had heard they don't teach penmanship as they used to. That is a mistake—all things must eventually fail. The old ways require no infrastructure to operate them."

Janet glared at him. "I'm doing the best I can. I'll be able to read it, and that's what counts."

Pleased at having teased her, he held his hands up. "Peace! I meant no disrespect. But you should practice writing more often. You would improve, and then everyone could read it, not just you."

Looking at her barely legible mess, Janet could only agree. Still, it wasn't fair that he sat there looking so innocent and serious, when clearly he was *not* innocent. "Okay. Who are you really?"

He nodded. "I've waited a long time for someone to ask me that question. It's the right question—the only one that matters. Autumn has come, and someone finally asks the question that matters." He smiled as she held her pen poised over the page, looking at him expectantly. "I'm Tam, son of Tam Lin and the Maab, the Fairy Queen. I was born in this house and lived here with my fairy mother until I was six. After Janet freed my father, my mother was advised by her court to send me to Oberon in his place as her tithe. Instead, she sent one of her courtiers and abandoned me on the doorstep of a childless couple. That was as much love as she would ever show anyone. Fairies don't raise half-mortal children, but my father didn't know this. He never knew my fate and probably assumed I had been taken to Faerie with the others."

Janet set the pen down, deciding to just leave since he was insisting on spinning a tale. "I thought you would be honest with me." She jumped as the quill rose of its own volition and hovered over the page, ready to take notes. Scowling, she said to the pen, "All right. You do it then." She crossed her arms and looked away from Tam. "And Tam was supposed to be sent to Hell as Maab's tithe, not to Oberon."

"You weren't there." He spoke sharply. "What do you know? I was there, and I'm telling you what really happened." Tam came around the table and sat beside her, willing her to look at him. "Look. I know it's difficult to believe. When I was grown and my foster mother had passed away, I returned to this house, looking for my mother. She was gone, and I've never seen her since. I wasn't surprised, as fairies never stay in one world for long.

"But the house remembered me and knew I was her heir. This house and these woods are my inheritance from my birth mother. The others have gone to the world they created, and I was left behind. I am half fairy—neither here nor there." He stopped, waiting for her response.

Janet watched Tam, her face stony. "Why are you insisting on this fantasy? If it were true, you would be in England or Europe, not America."

"This house and these woods are wherever they choose to be." Tam laughed, but it was bitter. "I was in Europe until recently. When I was suddenly granted a senior research fellowship at the university here, I knew something important was looming, but I didn't know what. How could I have known it was you?" His expression grew serious. "You need to be aware—this house does nothing that does not advance its purposes. I have no idea what it plans for you, any more than I know what it plans for me. And now—autumn is here. I knew summer was drawing to a close, but I thought I had more time."

Her eyes widened with alarm. "For me? What do you mean?"

His resigned tones worried her as much as his words. "You are here. You knocked, and the door swung open to admit you. A guest room has appeared, with amenities you will appreciate."

"Surely it won't hold me prisoner." Janet breathed the words, as if they were a prayer.

"I told you, I rarely have visitors. I didn't tell you how infrequently people find this place. The last guest I had was Francis James Child in the year 1851. He was young and obsessed with the Tam Lin tales, as he'd only just heard of them. After that, until recently, my interactions have only been allowed in European venues." He paused and then said, "I say interactions, but since Frank was here, no one has been allowed to walk these woods or visit my home until you, today. All of my contact with the outside world is through the crystal. I don't know why you have been brought here."

A world of fear was in her voice. "What are you going to do with me?"

He looked shocked. "I? Nothing, except be a proper host." Tam shook his head. Perhaps it was the firelight, lending his features a fleeting regret. "If you are done with me and my companionship, I will take you to your room where you may lock the door against me if you feel so inclined. Tomorrow after breakfast, I will try to lead you back to the path you strayed from, if I am allowed."

Sadness radiated from him, and despite her confusion and fear, she wanted to offer him some comfort. "I just need to think about things. This has been a long day, and many strange things have happened."

He just nodded, and rising, he said, "I'll bring your backpack if you like. I think you'll find your room has everything you could want."

True to his word, Tam left her in her room, with the large key in the lock on her side of the door. Heavy drapes were drawn over the windows, blocking any draft. Candles lit the room, a low fire burned, and a nightgown lay on the counterpane. A wardrobe held several skirts and blouses similar to what she had worn that day. Through a small doorway, she found a Victorian bath chamber, complete with a china chamberpot. She wondered if it emptied itself.

A slight sound made her jump, as if a branch rustled against her window. Leaves and small branches were blown against her windows as the wind began to howl, a windstorm announcing the arrival of autumn. Why did that thought make Tam so sad?

She had just managed to get comfortable in her bed when she heard a strange, low growl outside her window, followed by a snuffling sound. The window rattled slightly, as if someone was testing to see if it was locked. Then it rattled sharply, as someone tried to break in.

Blind, unreasoning terror gripped her, and without thinking, she leapt out of bed and ran to Tam's room, knocking on his door. "Something is trying to get into my room." She felt like weeping, standing there begging him for comfort when she had been so cold to him earlier. "Please, can you see what it is?"

Clad in his nightshirt, he opened the door, holding a sword. "I feared they would know you were here. Sleep in my bed. I'll sit up and keep watch."

Shivering, she entered his room. "They who? Not bears or wildcats. This was trying to get in the window."

"No. It was likely näcken. They too are creatures of Faerie, trapped in this realm as am I. Once they were merely mischievous, but summer has ended, and now they are changed. They've become...you wouldn't believe me if I told you what they've become, but please believe me when I say they're not safe." He drew back the covers for her and tucked her in. Then she watched as he sat in the chair, the sword across his knees. Her eyes closed, and at last she slept.

Tam watched Janet sleeping, lonelier than he'd ever felt in all his centuries of isolation. He spoke softly to the house, his only companion for more years than he wanted to remember. "Summer is over. All things must eventually die, and we are no exception. What will happen to you, dear house, when I am gone?" He gazed into the fire, where a face appeared within the flames, shrugging. He whispered, "It appears that Tam, Tam Lin's son, will die too, unbelieved and unloved. It is hard to think that just when I found her, this house and this world have reached the end of days."

Tam closed his eyes, listening, as all around the house, näcken gathered, testing every crack and cranny to see if they could get in.

He made up his mind. "Tomorrow she must go. She must not be here when winter comes. The time of the draugur is nearly upon us, the advent of the eternal night of Faerie. You, dear house, will crumble and we will die, as is the way of all things. But I should have liked to have known love."

The face in fire nodded and faded as the flames died down.

Sometime later Janet woke. Tam stood before the open window with his lute, singing. His music was powerful, and somehow she knew he sang a spell against the creatures that prowled outside the house. His voice rose and fell, captivating her.

It was then that she believed he was who he said he was, and it was then she realized she loved him. She loved both the beguiling fairy, Tam, and pale, ordinary Professor Thomlinsen, whose life force was stretched between two worlds. Beneath either disguise was a simple, lonely man she wanted to hold and comfort.

His voice died away, the diamond-paned window shut, and the drapes fell closed. Tam set his lute on a shelf and returned to the chair. He looked exhausted. "Autumn is passing, and winter is poised to take these woods. My magic is fading." The desolate look in his eyes broke her heart.

Janet sat up, her hair falling around her. She got out of bed and took his hand. "Come and hold me. I'll sleep better knowing I'm safe with you."

The firelight lent his features an unearthly grace, and her breath caught as he smiled. "Ah, but will you be safe? I'm both a fairy and a mortal man, and you are beautiful. Perhaps you shouldn't trust me to behave as a gentleman if we must share a bed."

In answer, she bent down and whispered, "I believe in you, Tam Lin, son of Tam Lin."

His arms went about her, strong but tender. Time stood still as Tam gently kissed her, and their world narrowed to a sharing of love, pure and honest.

The next morning Janet fidgeted, checking and rechecking her backpack. Tam insisted she go. "The näcken will never rest, knowing you're here. Winter has come, and my magic won't keep them at bay for much longer. I will speak with you through the crystal as long as I am able, I swear."

Unshed tears made her voice thick. "That is not a good solution."

Emotions he had no words for kept him from meeting her eyes. "There can be no other answer. I cannot leave this place."

Reluctantly she agreed but asked, "What does it mean, that winter is here?"

He told her the truth, unwillingly. "I am a fairy. We are summer people. In Faerie it is always summer, and the Fae live long, though not forever. But winter has come to my woods far sooner than I had hoped. I am not immortal, and my time is over."

She stood silent, unable to believe what he had just told her. "No. You can't die—I want to be here with you."

They jumped as a picture fell from the wall. He shook his head. "No. The house is dying, and I can't protect you. I am tied to the house and to the woods, so I must stay. I wish…I wish I'd found you before, while summer was still in these woods."

Tears filled her eyes, but she went to her room, washing her face and dressing.

While she made herself ready for the long walk, Tam walked around the clearing, seeing no leaves on the trees. The many small footprints made by the clogs worn by the näcken and some by creatures he didn't know were disturbing.

They had trampled his garden.

That they had been strong enough to pass through the wards around the plot was disturbing. "So many…they wanted her badly. I won't be able to stop them tonight. Will I become one of them in her stead?"

He desperately didn't want the näcken to take her. "The world turns and the seasons pass. Now is the dark time, the time for machines and madness. Winter has come—my time is ending."

When he turned to go back inside, he saw the roof of his house was covered with moss, and a shutter hung askew. His home had taken on a dilapidated, abandoned air. With shock, he realized his house was dying, far more rapidly than he believed. "I thought we had more time."

Inside, Janet sat before a low fire that tried to burn but did little to warm the house.

As he stood wondering what that low fire meant, Janet rose.

Breakfast appeared on the table, and they sat down to eat in silence, neither one able to say what was in their hearts.

As Tam steeled himself to lead Janet out of the woods and out of his life forever, the sound of a shutter falling off the house jarred him. At the same time, a page of paper and the quill appeared on the table, the quill writing slowly:

Your fairy life has ended, your mortal life begins. Beware the creatures that roam the shadows—make haste to your new world lest they catch you and keep you. Love will be your immortality.

Shocked, Tam stood, not sure what to do. As he did so, a brown knapsack appeared beside Janet's backpack on the bench by the door. Atop the knapsack lay his lute, securely strapped to it.

The pen lifted and with great difficulty wrote: *Go now and go quickly. Magic fades and all things must die.*

The fire died, and the candles guttered out. Stricken, Tam realized his house had sacrificed itself for him.

Janet looped her arms into her backpack and helped Tam with his. The look in his eyes was heartrending—he was heartbroken and afraid. "Tam…you don't have to leave with me. I'll still love you."

The house shuddered. The table collapsed, and grabbing Tam's hand, Janet pulled him outside. Overcome by disbelief, they stood in the clearing and watched as the house fell in on itself. Tam was speechless.

The clearing was silent, as if the forest held its breath. "Come on. We have to honor its last request." Janet began dragging him. "It said to hurry."

She could tell Tam was disoriented and knew the house meant more to him than merely a shelter. But he pulled himself together and began walking quickly, leading the way. The forest was winter-bare, the path clearly visible.

After a while of silent walking, Tam said, "I wonder what the future holds. I've never had to wonder that before."

Janet laughed. "We've a home in Littleton, small though it is, and jobs at the university—although there is no magic, and you'll have to suffer my cooking or learn to cook for yourself."

Tam squeezed her hand. "Your devices are magic. But will you still love me when the glamour is gone? When I leave these woods, I will be plain Tam Thomlinsen, professor of obscure and arcane literature no one else cares about. No magic and no great charm."

She smiled. "And I will be Janet Lund, the frumpy, studious MFA candidate who loves arcane things and eloped with her advisor, thus making everyone wonder what lurks beneath the surface of both of them."

Tam laughed as she hoped he would. Suddenly, a feeling of being watched by unfriendly eyes came over them. He said, "Näcken—they've become strong enough to endure the light of the winter sun. We must run." Gripping hands as they raced up the path, he led her through the barren woods. They leapt shallow creeks and stepped over fallen logs, sensing danger on their heels.

They neared the rim of the valley, but the path disappeared. Through the bare branches, they could see in the distance an autumn forest, the boundary sharply delineated. For a moment, Tam was unsure what to do, how to get there. The sounds of twigs snapping behind them spurred them on, and thorns caught at their clothes. Fearing they were lost, Tam had to hope for the best. Choosing a course, he plowed through the underbrush, but nothing was familiar. Panic made it impossible for him to know which way.

When he faltered, Janet gripped his hand, tugging him in the right direction, aiming for the golden larches she had seen the day before, sure now of why she had been blessed with that vision. Breathless and rapidly running out of strength, she dragged him through the brush. At last she saw it—a place where the air formed a wall that was almost like the surface of a pond.

"That is it," Tam said, hope and fear in his voice. "The border between the worlds."

Fear lent her strength, and Janet ran, drawing Tam toward the hazy green-gold of the autumn forest that was the mortal world. Desperately, winter fought to claim them. Ice formed beneath their feet, making their footing treacherous, and their breath burned their lungs and froze in clouds, but still they ran.

They were so close, so nearly there. Only a few yards....

Janet cried out in terror as twigs and thorns became gnarled hands that clawed at her skirts. Black talons clutched at Tam, trying to pull him from her grip, dragging him backward. "Janet—go. You must live. I love you!"

"No! They can't have you!" Janet gripped Tam's arm tightly, and from somewhere she found the power. Together they leapt...

...Into the warmth of a late September morning, bursting out of the shrubs onto the graveled path that circled the park, falling and rolling across the ground. Several bicycle riders swerved to avoid hitting them.

One young man stopped and assisted them to their feet, continuing on after being reassured they were fine.

The day was warm and the sky blue. Tam was silent, and Janet could see him wondering what would happen next, what she would think now that he was mortal.

Janet looked up at him. The glamour had gone, and he was no longer the charismatic fairy that took her breath away. Yet he was real, more substantial than Professor Thomlinsen had ever been, and she loved him. Throwing her arms around him she kissed him. "I love you, Tam, son of Tam Lin. Let's go home."

THE HOUSE IN THE WOODS
By Stephen Swartz

"Once upon a time there was a house in the woods: an old, abandoned house, fallen into disrepair and stuck deep in the dark middle of a foreboding wood, far away from polite society." That's the way I usually begin the story. Then I like to add: "And in that house there might be a dead body."

That's what I used to tell my friend Billy. He was a scaredy cat so anything I said made him nervous. The possibility of a dead body scared him the most. That was fun, getting him scared. His short blond hair would stand on end and sometimes he'd pee his pants. He really hated that house, especially, so I liked finding an excuse to go there. One day, we went inside.

Me and Billy would always go out exploring the woods near where we lived. It was the 60s and Mom would always shout at me, "It's such a nice day, why don't you go outside and play?" She really just wanted some time to herself. But I didn't mind. I'd go over to Billy's house and the two of us would find something to do. Grab a couple sticks off the ground and we could be Musketeers, sword fighting our way into the castle to save the princess. Or we could play Army. We were the American soldiers hunting for Nazis in the woods.

"Maybe some of them were hiding out in that old house," I suggested to Billy that Saturday afternoon.

"Why would any Nazi hide in that old house?" he asked. He looked at me with desperation, like *please don't make me go in there*.

"Where else they gonna hide?" I pointed to the house from where we hid behind a bunch of undergrowth. "You see that veranda and the broken steps? Nobody's gone up there for years. Look at them windows, too. They were broken even before my family moved here. Somebody threw rocks, I guess. Even the top window, up there in the attic, it's got a big crack in it."

"Just some older kids messin around," said Billy. "If a Nazi was gonna hide in there, everybody'd know where he was."

"Maybe." I rubbed my chin, acting like I was thinking. "Or, if everybody *guessed* the Nazi was in that house, then the Nazi would *think* that everybody would think that the Nazi would *know* everybody was thinking that, so nobody would even look in there. So the Nazi would hide there because nobody would think he would hide in there."

"Stop confusing me!" He started to get up from where we knelt. "I'm going home."

"Wait, Billy! What if the Nazis are watching us?"

He froze, then crouched down. "I don't think there're any real Nazis around here in these woods."

"Oh, they're all over. They escaped after the war, ya know, and now they could be living anywhere. They could be one of our neighbors."

Billy was a year younger than me, about twelve back then. But he seemed younger and I tried to act older. We always had a good time playing together, starting when his family moved into the house on my street, less than a mile from the edge of these woods.

It used to all be woods here, and some pasture land. There were horses grazing in the pasture when my family first moved here. The edge of suburbia, my dad said, only the woods beyond us. We had only half a street back then, until they started building houses on the other side and finished the street. Further down, the woods started, filled with oaks and hickory trees. I usually cut through those woods behind the next row of houses and hiked until I met the trail to the house coming from another direction.

Then Billy's family moved in. We were friends right from the start, being the only boys our age in the neighborhood. We rode the same bus to school, and when we weren't in school, we were with each other. Our moms didn't care where we went, just be home before dark and don't get bit by a rattlesnake. It was pretty boring because there was no rattlesnakes around there. At least, we never saw any.

"So we better make sure there's no Nazi hiding in there," I said, nudging Billy in the ribs with my elbow. "Or we better call the cops."

"I'm already sure nobody's in there."

"Well, maybe not *now*."

"What do you mean *not now*?"

"The Nazi could've died there. You know, while he was waiting for other Nazis to come and rescue him."

"We woulda seen it on the TV news."

"Not if it happened a long time ago." I cleared my throat. "See, if a Nazi had escaped from Germany way back then and he was found out over here, then he probably had to hide in these woods. And if he found this house, he would hide in it."

"Then how would he die?"

"He stayed there waiting for help and he starved. He couldn't go out to get food or people'd see him. So he just starved to death."

"*Wow*. You think so?"

"Probably." I faced the house, staring through the bushes. "Yessiree, his body's still sitting in a chair, I bet. Waiting for help to arrive. Nothing but skeleton now."

Billy shivered, even though it was a hot summer afternoon. "Come on, let's go."

"You mean go inside?"

"No, go *home*. It's getting late. Mom said not to be late."

"Late for what?"

"For…getting home."

I glared at him, and he knew I caught him lying. I patted him on the shoulder. "You gotta start being braver, Billy. Stop being a baby. The world's not full of scary things like you think."

"Yea, I know."

I stood, pulling him up with me, my hand on his arm.

"We got our sticks, so we're safe. Let's see what's really in there," I said.

"Are you sure?"

"Listen, Billy. It's just an old abandoned house in the middle of the woods. Probably nobody lived there for decades—or centuries, even. Anything bad would've left already. And nobody knows it's even here, still standing."

"Maybe it's like private property. We shouldn't go in."

"If it was private property, they'd put up a sign."

He stared at the house, thinking about laws and stuff. "I guess…."

"Then let's go."

We stepped slowly forward, like we expected someone to shout from the house for us to get off their property. We had to stop a couple times to listen. The wind rattling the leaves of the trees made it hard to hear if anybody was shouting at us. Billy got behind me, and I led the way up the grassy walk that had once been covered with flat stones, up to the broken steps.

Billy was grabbing the back of my belt so tight I couldn't take another step forward.

"Let go," I snapped at him. "We're almost there."

I continued and put my foot on the first crumbling step. Two stone steps then wooden ones. The wood was broken, like somebody too heavy for it tried to go up them. I stepped up along the side of the steps.

When I got up on the veranda, I stopped and looked back at Billy. He was still on the grass. I waved at him to get on up here, gritting my teeth like I was mad at him. He stumbled up the steps and stood beside me in a flash.

"Shhh," I said, holding my finger to my lips. "You sure do make a lotta noise."

I took a couple steps to the front door. It was closed, but I saw it didn't hang even, so it was easy to push it open and let it swing back against the inside wall. We could see the living room clear as day. The furniture was still there but in terrible shape. They weren't even covered in sheets like you see in the movies.

"Look at that," I said. "They didn't even move out, just left it all like this."

"So...maybe they're coming back? Someday?"

"Yea, maybe *today*." I laughed.

"Stop it! You're scaring me." He swatted at my shoulder.

"Nothing to be scared of, Billy. Besides, we got our sharp sticks in case we get attacked."

"I don't wanna be attacked."

"Then *Shut. Up.*"

We stepped into the house, watching our sneakers so we didn't land on any creaking floor boards. We didn't want anybody to hear us and come running out demanding we get off this property. Or something worse, like a rabid raccoon or such.

The living room used to have a rug. It was rolled up against the far wall, leaving the floor boards exposed. They were all scratched and rough. Straight ahead was a stone fireplace. To the left was a high-back upholstered chair, something like Dad sat in at home to read his newspaper. To the right was a couch with the cushions missing. There was a dark stain on it, where people's backs would be if they sat on the couch. I pointed to it.

"Could be blood," I said. "Maybe there was a murder."

Billy was shivering again. I could feel it through the floorboards under my feet.

We got inside far enough that we could look both ways and see more of the house. To the left was the dining room and beyond was a door leading into the kitchen, I guessed. In the dining room there was still a big table with one broken dining chair on its side on the floor. A chandelier that used to hang from the ceiling had fallen on top of the table so there were hundreds of little glass pieces everywhere. To the right in the living room, we saw a staircase leading up to the second floor. Covering everything were streams of cobwebs, and the little sunlight that shone through the grimy windows lit up the cobwebs like tinsel on a Christmas tree.

"I don't see no Nazi here," said Billy. "We better go now."

"If there's no Nazi here, then it's okay for us to be here, right?"

"What if they're hiding upstairs? What if they heard us and they're getting ready to attack?"

"Calm down, Billy. If they wanted to attack us, they'da done it already. You know, they can just shoot down through the floor and we'd be dead already."

We both looked up at the ceiling. Peeling wallpaper. Cracks. Mildew. No bullet holes.

"I seen enough," said Billy.

"A house this size gotta have some secrets. Come on."

I made my way to the stairs and up to the second floor, each step causing a creak. At the top was a hallway with doors on each side. The doors were all closed. At the end of the hallway was a half-open door. I guessed from what I could see that it was a bathroom.

When I took my first step from the top stair onto the hallway floor, there was a loud creak. Billy stumbled back down the stairs a couple, caught his breath. I looked back at him, waved my hand for him to come on up.

"There could be a Nazi in one of them bedrooms," I whispered to Billy when he was beside me at the top of the stairs.

He was shaking. "You're not gonna open them, are you?"

"How you gonna know what's inside if you don't open the doors?"

"I don't wanna know what's inside, to be perfectly honest."

"Yeah, you're perfectly honest, all right." I laughed and he grabbed my arm. I pushed him off me. "That's me laughing, you dope. Not the Nazi."

Billy simpered a bit, slapping my arm. "Stop teasing me! You're always doing that."

"I bet there's a Nazi in one of them bedrooms. You know, the one that starved to death. He just got too weak, ya know, so he laid down to sleep and never woke up. Just died like that."

"You think?"

"Oh, yeah, it's possible. By now he'd be a skeleton inside a uniform." My face brightened. "Maybe he had a gun with him. Maybe it's still there beside his body. Maybe in his cold, dead hand. We should get it."

"Well, I'm not goin' in there!"

"You don't have to, Billy. Just open the door and look in. You can stay in the hallway."

"I'm not even gonna do that."

"Hey, here's four bedrooms. A dead Nazi's gotta be in one of them."

"But which one?"

"And who would be in the other bedrooms?" I wondered.

"Who else is gonna be here with a Nazi?"

"Maybe his girlfriend. Or maybe some people he kidnapped. Like he made them come here like hostages. They do that kind of thing, ya know."

We looked at each other. Could be true, our eyes seemed to say. My mind was working overtime to put ideas into Billy's head. I saw it was working. He was about to cry. I didn't think there was any Nazis hiding in the house, but Billy was falling for it. If I could get him to pee his pants, it would be a great day!

"Okay, I'll open the door on the right and you open the door on the left. That way, if any Nazi jumps us the other one of us can help fight him."

"I'm not opening any door."

"Come on, scaredy cat. You wanna be brave, don't cha?"

"I guess so."

"Then you gotta do it."

I pushed him forward, ahead of me. We took a few steps up to the first pair of doors, opposite each other along the hallway. I stood in front of my door, and Billy got in front of his door. I put my hand on the doorknob. I looked back over my shoulder, glaring at Billy until he took hold of the doorknob of his door.

Ready? I mouthed. *On three.* I held up my fingers: one…two… *three!*

Billy turned the doorknob and the door opened with a long creak. He jumped back, bumping into me. I didn't open my door because I was watching to make sure Billy opened his. But when he bumped into me, I slammed forward against my door with a loud *wham* that would let anybody in the house know that intruders were present.

"Watch it!" I barked at Billy. "Now they know for sure we're here."

We turned to look at Billy's door. It was open about four inches. We could see some waving lights—a few branches of the trees outside playing with the sunlight, I guessed. But to Billy, it was a sure sign of ghosts. He almost hugged me in his fright.

"Get off me!" I said, pushing him away.

"There're ghosts in there."

I explained about curtains and branches and sunlight to this stupid kid.

"Oh," he responded.

"Now let's go in and take a look."

Inside was an ordinary bedroom. Looked like for a girl. A bed and dresser with a girly style. The wallpaper was pink and had little white ponies all over it. I guessed this house used to be a farm house, and the land around it was the farm. Then whatever happened made the family leave. But they didn't take any furniture with them. Even the bed still had sheets on it. And a pillow. It was all covered in a layer of gray dust, though.

"Nap time!" I called to Billy. "Go lay down there."

"Not me. Are you crazy?"

"It's just dust," I said.

He leaned forward to get a better look.

"But you know most dust in a house is just dead skin flakes. That's probably what all that covering the sheet is. Dead skin."

He leaned back away from the bed. I thought he was about to pee.

"And look at that spot," I said. "Down there on the sheet. Is that a pee stain? It's about where a pee stain would be if somebody was laying there and peed while they slept."

Billy looked again. "Stop talking about peeing. I gotta go now."

"There's a bathroom down at the end of the hallway."

"I'm not going there by myself."

"You want me to watch you pee?"

"No, just stand outside in case the Nazi comes."

I nodded. "Looks like no Nazi in this room. Maybe this was the room where the little girl was sleeping when the Nazi killed her and took her body away. Maybe we should look for graves in the back yard."

"Cut it out!"

"Yea, the Nazi probably cut out her tongue so she wouldn't say nothing about him."

"I mean stop scaring me!"

"I'm not scaring you. I'm not scaring anybody, just thinking what maybe happened in this house."

Billy stepped toward the door. "I really gotta pee now."

"So let's go to the bathroom. I'll watch you pee. And make sure you wash your hands."

"Shut up!"

We stepped lightly down the hallway to the open door, still afraid to be noisy, and, yes, that room was a bathroom. Billy went in first, halting suddenly. I stood behind him, looking over his shoulder. The bath tub, we saw, was filled with something brown, like a liquid never drained out. A few flies were buzzing around. It stunk real bad.

"What's that?" asked Billy.

"Somebody was really dirty."

"That can't be just what washed off somebody."

"Maybe the Nazi cut everybody up and tried to wash the blood away but it clogged up the drain. You know pieces of skin and organs'll clog up a drain."

"Doesn't look like blood. It's brown, too."

"And don't smell too good, neither."

"Did somebody take a crap in the tub?"

"Nope. Not that much, anyway. Could be dried blood. You know it does turn kinda brown after a while."

I glanced over at the toilet. The lid was down.

"You said you needed to pee? There's the toilet."

Billy glared at me like I was daring him. He didn't want to touch it, not even to lift the lid. We both seemed to wonder what might be in there, looking up at us when we lifted the lid.

"Maybe it's one of the Nazi's victim's heads," I said and shoved Billy forward.

He scrambled back. "You open it."

"I thought you was the one that wanted to pee."

"Just open it."

"Use your stick," I said. After all, that's why boys carry sticks, especially sharpened ones, for anything that might need to be poked or pried open.

He worked the point of his stick into the gap between the ceramic basin and the wooden seat and lifted them until they flipped back against the water tank with a big *clunk*. We both craned our necks to look into the toilet. It was dry, no water, just ugly, gross red stains. Probably rust, but I told Billy it could be blood.

"No it's not."

"Could be," I said. "So go ahead and pee already."

"I can't just pee into an empty toilet."

"You're not gonna flush it anyway. There's no water. It's been off for a long time."

We both seemed to get the same idea and turned to the bath tub.

"I'll pee into the tub."

"So go ahead."

"Well, I can't do it with you watching."

I threw my hands up. "Okay, I'll step outside."

"But not too far."

I backed out of the bathroom, and when I turned around to look down the hallway, a brilliant idea came into my head.

I decided to hide from Billy. He would panic and go searching for me. He would have to open every door looking for me. That would make him learn how to be brave.

So I returned to the first door that I was supposed to open, but instead I watched Billy open his. I turned the doorknob and opened the door. I knew there wasn't any Nazis hiding in this house in the woods. I was not a scaredy cat like Billy. I wasn't afraid of anything—except real stuff, like if a wolf came out of the woods and attacked me. Stuff like that. I wasn't afraid of anything imaginary.

The room I entered was dark, no sunlight on this side of the house. But there was enough of a leak around the window curtains that I could see the room was probably the parents' bedroom. A double-sized bed sat there, also with sheets and pillows, also covered in years of dust, also gross. But I wasn't gonna take a nap on it, anyway.

I looked around for a place to hide. Under the bed? Too dirty. Behind the bed—on the far side between the bed and the wall? Or in the closet?

I went to the closet and swung open the door as freely as if it was my own closet back home, not expecting anything to jump out and grab me.

Inside were a few clothes on hangers, women's dresses mostly. One looked like a wedding dress. A man's suit, black like for a funeral, also hung there. Nobody left clothing and bedding and furniture when they moved away, I thought. That was when I first wondered what happened to the family that had lived. Why did they leave so quickly without packing up their things?

Maybe they went on a trip and were killed in an accident and so they never came home again. But then there would be more things still in the house, in the rooms, in the closets. Not just these few things that seemed to be selected to stay while they took other things. Maybe they thought the house was haunted so they just left one day. Maybe there really was a Nazi, or some crazed criminal, who ran through these woods and came upon this house and decided to trick the family into taking him in, giving him food, a place to rest a while. Nice people do that.

Then they get paid back.

I heard Billy calling me. His voice was excited, worried. I

almost called back out of habit, but I wanted to scare him real good this time. So I got inside the closet, stood between the hanging clothes, and reached out to close the door. I didn't close it all the way. Then he might not check it. I left it open about an inch, enough to make him curious.

And I waited.

I could hear Billy walking down the hallway, the floor boards squeaking and creaking with each step. He kept calling my name, but each time his voice sounded weaker, like he wasn't sure I was even in the house any longer. I had to practically bite my tongue to keep from answering him. I was getting nervous, too, hoping my prank would pay off bigtime. Since he already peed, maybe he would dirty his pants. That would be even greater!

The doorknob to this bedroom rattled. The door swung open with another long creak.

"George?" he called softly, like he didn't want anybody but me to hear him.

He stepped further into the room. *Creak...creak* across the wooden floorboards. I remembered the position of everything in the room. He was at the bed, maybe got down to look under it. *Creak...creak* back across the room. I sensed he was looking at the closet door, wondering what to do. I readied myself to pounce on him when he opened the closet door.

Reach for it, Billy, reach for the doorknob.

He opened it.

"*Yeehaaaaaaaah!*" I shrieked as I jumped out at him.

Then something felt strange. I thought I was falling on top of Billy, both of us down on the floor. But not the way I thought it would be. He was scared, for sure. I saw it in his eyes that first instant. I did not know if he dirtied his pants, but I felt something wet between us.

I rolled off him and my hand went to my chest. Pulling my hand back, I saw it was covered with blood. Not old brown blood like we saw in this house but fresh red blood that was pouring out of me like from a garden hose.

Billy got up, rolled up onto one knee, staring down at me. He looked half scared and half...*satisfied?*

Then he pulled out the stick from my chest. More blood spurted. My first thought was we better do something quick or I would die. I remembered how blood worked. If you lost too much of it you died.

I gazed up at Billy. "What…?"

"Not scared now, huh." His face was cold. "I told you not to scare me."

"I didn't sc—"

I couldn't breathe, and the room began swirling like I was on a carnival ride. Yeah, we shoulda gone to the carnival today, not gone exploring some old house in the woods. That was just plain stupid.

I saw my blood spreading out across the floor as Billy stood tall over me.

All I could think was that he probably would've realized his predicament in the next few minutes. He would go home, but then questions about his friend would be asked. He would say he didn't see me today, that we never met up to play in the woods. Maybe the grownups would figure out something, needing to solve the mystery, and go looking for me.

They likely would've followed the same trail me and Billy followed. That would lead them to this old abandoned house. They probably would've searched it like we did. They would check each room, look in each closet. But they would not find any bodies. Not even a Nazi body.

That was because Billy found a place where the floorboards were loose in the living room, and he could slide them off and dig a hole there to hide my body in. To make it stay put, he returned with some nails and hammered the floorboards down tight. Then he scrubbed the blood on the bedroom floor and unrolled the living room rug over the bedroom floor.

Eventually, he forgot about me, stopped visiting the house just to stomp on the floor over me. I'm sure he went on to high school, got a good job like his dad, and maybe had a family—a family like the one that lived in this house before. And he probably never told anyone about what happened that afternoon in the summer of 1966. He never told anyone about his friend George, who vanished one day, except perhaps to offer one possibility that he had been kidnapped by a biker gang and killed later, in another state. And that was all anyone knew.

Now I live in the house in the woods.

And no one visits me.

THE GUARDIAN
By Irene Roth Luvaul

Helen was bent over in her garden, weeding and tending to two little trees that had just taken a growing spurt, when a deer leaped over the fence, startling her, and then stopped right in front of her. She stood straight up and gawked at the deer that stared back at her with wide, startled eyes. Then it stepped forward and put its head against her, and she felt it tremble.

What an odd thing, Helen thought, as she slowly moved away. Never had a deer—and lots of them roamed around her cottage in the forest—approached her like that. Its eyes moved to look at something behind her, and then it bolted away in the opposite direction, jumping the fence once again.

Unnerved, Helen picked up her tools and walked back toward her house. Dark shadows passed over her and across the walkway. When she looked through the trees rising up before her, she saw buzzards circling almost directly above. Worried now, she turned and walked from her yard toward the thicket of trees, scanning the ground ahead of her.

When she entered the denser part of the forest, she gagged as the stench of death overwhelmed her. She moved slowly, reluctantly, toward the source of the odor and came to a small clearing. There, the body of some animal lay, dismembered, blood clotted, decomposing – another deer.

Maybe that's what was going on with that other deer, she thought as she hurried back toward home. But as she got closer to her yard, more alert this time, she found other bodies, smaller ones, some mutilated, some only bloody, but all dead: a squirrel, a rat, a tiny shrew. *What in the world?*

Helen had noticed little things happening lately, strange things – now, these dead bodies. Earlier that day, two birds had landed on her shoulder as she turned the key in the door to her home, and as they fluttered their wings against her neck, she felt the drumming of their little hearts. Then, as suddenly as they had appeared, they darted up into the air and flew straight into the forest.

Now, shaking her head, she walked back to her garden, trying to calm down, wondering what had happened to the animals. She stopped beside the two trees she'd found a few years ago deep in the forest, in a glen so hidden away that, try as she might, she'd never been able to find it again. The scent of those trees, so sharp, so spicy, had reminded her of the smell of the wood her house had been built with. She had dug them up and transplanted them near her house, watching them grow, caring for them. As always when she worked in her garden, she began to calm down, but then she heard the phone ringing in her kitchen, and she ran to answer it.

It was her building contractor with some questions. "Yes," she said, "there's so much more room, and I love that I now have windows. What? Oh, the cabinet. Yes, if you don't mind, please store it there at your place. I'll decide what to do with it later. Really? I didn't realize that. The bottom of it was actually a part of an old tree stump under the house? How weird. Well, again, just keep it there and I'll call you when I figure out what to do with it."

Helen had arranged for the back room to be renovated because she wanted an office that looked out on the forest, and the location of that room was perfect, except it had had no windows and was too dark. Helen was a fairly successful writer and had written most of her fantasy novels sitting at the huge, wooden table in the kitchen. Now that she was a bit famous and made a little extra money, she wanted a writing sanctuary worthy of a great novelist. She always thought that with a little self-effacing grin on her face.

After she hung up the phone, she walked into the still-empty room that smelled of fresh sawdust and paint, and she twirled around slowly, her arms outstretched. Plenty of room here, she thought. But then she stopped and realized she would miss that enormous cabinet after all. She remembered stories her grandmother told to her mother and then her mother to her, stories of a great-great-grandfather lost to time, who had built this house from the very wood that had grown where the house now sat. The wood had been hacked from huge maples and evergreens and some species of tree she'd never been able to find any information about, something her mother had called a guardian tree. The massive stumps still surrounded the house, stumps that Helen had played king-of-the-world on as a little girl. And she remembered the story about the cabinet, now gone, about how that grandfather had built and carved it from the largest, oldest tree in the forest, but she'd never been told that the cabinet was actually still attached to the base of that old tree, still a part of it.

Although it had always been called a cabinet, there was no discernable door, so, short of taking an ax to it, there was no way to open it. As far as she knew, no one had ever discovered its original purpose.

Helen left the room, closing the door, and then stopped suddenly. She just realized that the weird things that had begun to happen – the strange actions of that deer, the birds, the animals – those horrid dead animals – and, oh yes, Flee appearing more often – had happened since the contractors finished remodeling the room and removed the cabinet.

Maybe...oh, come on, Helen, she thought, shaking her head and laughing a little at herself, and then she turned to begin making plans to buy furniture for this wonderful new room where she would write many more books and spend her time peering out that big bay window, gazing out into her garden and the forest.

That night before going to bed, Helen walked toward the back room and started to reach for the light switch. But before her hand could find it, she felt something brush against her face, her hand, something cold, vile. She gasped and pulled her hand back. *What the–*. She quickly reached again and flipped the switch. Light filled the room. Nothing. The room was empty, the new windows looking out onto darkness.

Later, as Helen lay asleep in bed, night moving toward morning, a soft rustling roused her, and she sat bolt upright in bed. Dawning light came through the windows, shadows painting the usual patterns against the wall. She saw an apparition hovering at the foot of her bed, and sighing loudly, she lay back heavily on the mattress. "You again?" she said. "Go away, Flee," and she rolled over on her side.

The house was haunted. Everyone knew that. On her mother's lap on stormy nights, Helen had heard the story of Flee, the ghost who floated about the house at night, sometimes during the day, softly whispering words no one in her family could ever make out.

Flee, as the apparition had always been called, the reason lost to history, had appeared to her family for decades, centuries maybe. And when Helen, an only child, had left for college and then worked in the city for a few years, Flee was still there when she returned to her childhood home to write full time. Now, with her mother and father both gone, the beautiful cottage set back among the trees belonged only to her, and so apparently did this often-annoying ghost.

Sometimes as a child, while she played in the forest, jumping up on the old, rotting stumps, she imagined she had seen other apparitions like Flee and tried to talk to them. But they would never answer and would eventually disappear.

Even as an adult on her walks deep into the forest, prisms of rain from a recent storm dripping onto her head and shoulders from the towering trees above, she sometimes thought she glimpsed from the corner of her eye one of the specters hovering just above the ground. They had no substance but were wisps that seemed to sway in the wind, gleam in the sunlight. She was sure that if she could look directly at them, they would have faces, maybe even smiles since they seemed harmless, but when she turned to try to look at one, it seemed to evaporate.

Because she'd grown up in these woods and had explored the house inside and out, she should have been able to convince herself that the apparitions were just playthings invented by a little girl raised in a lonely cottage in the woods, real playmates many miles away in town. But she was not the only one to see Flee, to mention that she thought she saw other phantoms in the woods. Her family had always been convinced they actually existed, that their house, their forest, was haunted. What the specters were, what their purpose was, if there was one, was unknown and unfathomable, or maybe just lost in time like her old great-great-grandfather.

But now as Helen tried to wriggle back into sleep, Flee again made that rustling sound. Helen, eyes still closed, said, "Please go away." But she could still feel her presence, and when she opened her eyes, she cried out sharply. Flee was now standing closer to her, at the side of the bed, less of a specter now, seeming more solid, looking down at her. Tall, beautiful, elegantly strange, with long, dark hair to her waist, skin the color of cream, she appeared very real. The smell of the forest lay thick in the room, something earthy, ancient.

"You must return the Guardian," Helen heard her say, and she shook her head and rubbed her eyes, trying to decide if she'd really heard that, really seen that, or if she was in the middle of a dream.

"You are indeed awake, Helen. You are in danger, so too the animals." Flee was not talking in the usual sense but communicating some other way.

"You're real? You know my name?" Helen asked, shivering with something not so much like fear, but bewilderment.

"I appear real right now, yes. And yes, of course I know your name. I don't live in the same time as you, but in the same place. I'm always here. I've always been here."

Should I get out of bed? Is this thing dangerous? Have I lost my mind?

"Please. I'm not dangerous, but you are in danger. You must get up and return the Guardian." Flee shimmered now and seemed to fade, no longer as substantial.

Helen squinted at her. "Guardian?"

"Yes, without the Guardian, the Quayloon has escaped. Removing the Guardian has allowed this." Flee seemed to become more anxious and then her image flickered, disappearing and then reappearing, becoming again more tangible.

"Okay, wait. I'm getting up." To herself, Helen wondered if she should just dress and leave the room, hoping this...this ghost would be gone when she came back.

"I'm not a ghost. I'm as substantial right now as you."

Helen, totally confused and freaked out because the thing was reading her mind, said, "May I touch you, you know, just to be sure you are real and that I am not insane?"

Flee bent over and laid her hand on Helen's shoulder, smiling a sad smile. "I am real."

Helen stood up and faced her, no less agitated because the ghostly creature did seem real, at least when she'd touched her. "I'm sorry, Flee, but I don't understand."

Laughing softly, the apparition standing before her said, "I love the name your kindred have given me. My name is Flidais," which she pronounced as Flee-ish, "but your family has called me Flee for centuries. And I know you don't understand. We need to replace the Guardian, but it will take some time to explain so you will believe me. May we please begin?"

Helen stood up, pulling on a robe, and glanced at Flee. "Do you...?" She was going to ask Flee if she wanted a cup of coffee, but her voice trailed off.

"No, thank you. We Folk have no need to consume anything."

Folk? Helen thought to herself but aloud said, "Okay, but if I have to start the morning off talking to...whatever you are...*I* need a cup of coffee." She walked toward her kitchen, assuming Flee would follow. As she glanced back, Flee was in fact following her, but she wasn't walking. She was floating.

"Okay. I'm going to make this coffee, and then I need to sit down. I also need *you* to sit down because you floating around like that is freaking me out."

Though her face was still drawn, sad, Flee made a little sound that sounded like a chuckle. She hovered at the kitchen table, looking at the computer and stacks of books and paper the result of Helen's work. "A fantasy writer," Flee said, a statement, not a question.

"A fantasy writer, yes."

"You should have a good amount of material after this conversation, I imagine."

Helen smirked a bit and said, "Yeah, I think you might be right about that. I have been trying to come up with another story. Maybe this will be it." When the coffee was done, she held her cup with both hands, blowing across the top and then sipping slowly, and looked directly at her visitor. "Okay. What's a kwaloon, and what's the guardian? And what exactly are you?"

"All in good time." Flee stopped floating, settled into the chair Helen always sat in to work, and started her story.

"The Folk have always been here, I've always been here, and so also has the Quayloon. We live in a different dimension, a different time, but in the same place as you. The forest and the trees have always been our home. The sightings you have, those your family have had, of apparitions, of ghosts, as you think of them, are actually sightings of the Folk. We try not to be seen, but sometimes we fail.

"For eons, we have lived in the forest, unseen and in peace, unless something happens to awaken the Quayloon, to allow its escape. I am the caretaker of the animals and woodlands and have been able to control the Quayloon with the help of the Guardians."

While the story continued, Helen noticed that the table began to shake, her coffee splashing over the top of the cup. Flee's eyes grew wide, and her image began to waiver. Then she disappeared.

"Well, crap," Helen said out loud, pinching her arm to make sure she wasn't dreaming. Just as she stood up to get something to wipe up the coffee, Flee reappeared and began to continue with her story.

Helen slammed her palm on the table. "No! You're going to tell me what just happened."

"It was the Quayloon. Let me finish my story. What just happened is a warning of why you must return the Guardian."

Chastened and confused, Helen sat back down and picked up her coffee cup, rubbing at the small puddle of coffee on the table with the sleeve of her robe.

"The Quayloon ravages the animals of the forest, trying to deplete it, trying to make the forest itself die. Certain trees that grew only in this forest, Guardians, were the only things able to hold the Quayloon prisoner. Since they are all dead, since they no longer exist, the Quayloon is free to murder the animals of this forest and eventually all the other animals of Earth, including humans. The only beings that would be left are those like me, the Folk, who have no real substance and have no need to consume. But then the Folk would have no purpose, no animals to protect, no forests in which to live.

"For centuries, I was able to hold the Quayloon because the Guardians were numerous. But over the years, they began to grow old and some died. If dying of old age was the only problem, more than enough Guardians existed to hold the Quayloon. But centuries ago, civilization came to this part of the world, and because the trees, especially the huge Guardians, were there for the taking, humans began to cut them down. They built homes and bridges and buildings and developed the open spaces around the forest and then began to go right into the forest itself. Soon, only a very few Guardian trees were left. The largest of those that were left grew where your house now sits.

"One day about two centuries ago, a young man and his family arrived as I was surveying the forest and coming to grips for the first time with just how depleted the Guardians were. The new family set up a temporary camp just at the edge of the forest and began to make plans to build their home back into the forest. That young man was your kin, a grandfather of yours.

"As the days passed, I watched over that family, not only to be sure of their safety but also to be sure that the forest was safe. My priority was to keep that largest of the Guardians secure.

"The young man, William, often carried an ax with him as he foraged through the forest for food and firewood. The ax didn't concern me because it was much too small to do any real damage to the Guardian. But soon, he brought in more men to help him clear an area and harvest trees for wood to build his new home.

"I approached him one day as he was craning his neck, looking up into the air, inspecting the Guardian near his campsite. 'Do you intend to cut this tree?' I asked out loud, not using my mind to converse with him as I am doing with you now.

"William jumped backward and tripped over a tree root and fell to the ground. I had appeared to him as I appear to you now.

"'Jesus, Mary, and Joseph!' he cursed, as he stood up, brushing off the seat of his pants. 'Who...where did you come from?'

"'I am Flidais, caretaker of this forest.'

"'Flee-ish...what? Caretaker?' William quickly crossed himself. 'What manner of devil is this?'

"'William, I am no devil. I am, as I said, the caretaker of this forest. I demand that you not harm this tree in any manner.

"'How do you know my name? Demand? This is my legal homestead, you...whatever you are. I have every right and every intention of cutting this tree. I don't need the likes of you to take care of the forest, *my* forest.' He pulled off his hat, wiping the back of his hand across his forehead. 'Go back to whatever hell you came from.' He crossed himself again and walked back to his camp.

"But I followed him. 'Please, William, don't cut down this tree. It holds an evil presence. You'll rue the day you release it if you cut it down. It's a Guardian tree, protecting the forest, the animals, and now you, from the Quayloon, an entity that thrives on death, that wants to kill everything.'

"'Leave this place, Flee or whatever the devil your name is,' William shouted. 'I'll do as I please for me and my family. You and your evil presence begone!' Hearing those words and realizing that I would not be able to convince him this way, I began to fade then disappeared, though I was still nearby. 'Hey, where did you go?' William asked, and then he merely shrugged and shook his head. But he stood and stared for a long time at the place from which I had disappeared."

As Flee hesitated in her story, Helen heard an animal scream and bolted up from her chair, knocking it over and spilling the rest of her coffee. Flee again disappeared, and Helen righted her chair, wiped up the coffee, then sat down and put her head in her hands, waiting. "Another dead animal," Flee said when she reappeared. "I desperately need to secure the Quayloon, but I have no place to keep him now that the Guardian is not here."

"Then, damn it, where is the Guardian? What happened to it?" Helen was heartbroken that yet another animal was killed.

"You had it moved. But I must continue with my story so you will understand." And so she continued.

"A few days after confronting William, I was startled by a resounding thud, an immense tremble in the earth. The Folk were frightened, flitting around the forest, unable to avoid showing themselves. I knew immediately that the Guardian near William's camp had fallen. I appeared at the site, floating above the fallen tree as the morning sunlight shone through the forest. 'What have you done?' I asked.

"'I have harvested this tree, as is my right, to use for my family's home,' William said, his hand resting on the part of the Guardian remaining in the ground, his hand tiny against the span of that huge stump. The rest of the tree lay on the forest floor, dead. The men who had helped him fell the tree, kill it, terrified of whatever just appeared before them, turned and ran away.

"'You've loosed something that I must now restrain and capture, if I'm able. Without the Guardian, that may be impossible. You and your family are not safe here. You must leave until I am able to secure the Quayloon.' I knew it would soon begin to kill every living thing, now that it was free.

"'Leave? I have been working day and night to build something for my family, and you come here believing you have the right to tell me to leave? You are trespassing–'

"'William,' I said, interrupting him and spreading my arms wide to indicate the whole of the forest and pointing to the tops of the trees, 'this forest, this land, that tree, these trees, have been held by my people, the Folk, for eons. I am not trespassing. I'm trying to keep you and your family safe.'

"Before I could say more, William's wife came running up to us, screaming. She stopped abruptly, glancing in my direction, and stepped back a bit. Then she shrieked, 'He's gone, Will. I can't find him. He was just playing by the tent, and now he's gone.' And then she shouted her child's name. 'Aaron!'

"William picked up his ax. 'Come on, Ella. We'll find him.'

"I knew they would never find Aaron alive. 'Please take your wife and your men and leave this place. I need to capture the Quayloon and can't while all of you are in danger.'

"'Get out of here. I've got to find my boy.' He turned and followed his wife.

"I knew there was nothing I could do, not right then, to help William. He wouldn't leave before he found his son. I was afraid all he would find was his body. I knew the Quayloon well enough to know it would attack the first animal or human that crossed its path. I was certain that had been Aaron.

"William's wife, Ella, ran up to me. 'Can you help us? William told me you said you were a spirit or something. Can't you do anything? Please find my son. Please.'

Helen became frustrated with the lengthy story Flee seemed insistent on telling, even though animals were dying all around her home and the forest. "Please hurry up and finish. Obviously, something happened to that man's son and you did something to save him."

"No, I wasn't able to save him," she said, shaking her head, fading a bit. "The Quayloon killed him, along with William's beloved hunting dog and all of the livestock he had brought with him. He and his wife ended up with nothing but the pieces of the Guardian tree he had killed."

"So what happened then? Don't you have to hurry? Shouldn't you be doing something other than telling me ancient stories?" Helen stood up and paced, running her fingers through her hair.

"Of course I should be, but I have to make you realize it is now *you* who need to let me do my work. And I need you to return the Guardian you have because there is no other. So let me continue with William's story so that you'll understand what I need you to do.

"When William found Aaron's mutilated, bloody body deep in the forest, he carried him to me and gently laid him down on the ground at my feet. His eyes were puffy, and tears rolled down his face. Ella ran up, glanced at the child, and when she realized he was dead, she began to violently pummel William's chest but didn't say a word. She didn't cry, she didn't scream.

"William grabbed her and held her close. Over her head, he looked at me and said, 'What the hell are you? What is this kwaloon? What have you done?'

"'You must help me, William, so no one else is harmed. It's too late for your boy, but you must think of your wife, yourself.'"

Flee looked at Helen now and said, "I'm not human but know that humans feel loss so terribly. I feel the loss of the animals in my forest, the loss of humans who inhabit it, but I cannot fathom what the loss of one's own child must feel like." Then she looked away and continued with her story.

"Days went by. As now, the animals of the forest were being killed. The stench of death was thick in the air, and only the buzzards thrived, constantly circling above then diving down to feast on whatever the Quayloon had left. It was trying to kill everything until it was the only thing left, as it had always wanted to be. I was unable to find a single other Guardian, though I'm certain I searched the entire forest. William had felled the very last one.

"Then one day, he finally called to me at the forest's edge. When I appeared, he fell to his knees. 'Ella is leaving me unless I can stop this. She says it's my fault, that you warned me not to cut the tree. I might be able to make her stay if I can help stop this murdering, this killing of everything.'

"Although I wasn't certain it would work, William and I devised a plan to have the wood from the Guardian cut into planks. Then he'd use them to construct his home around the stump of the Guardian. Since I wasn't able to find a living tree to hold the Quayloon, he would carve a cabinet, a cell, into the stump, one without any access, and more importantly, without an exit. I wasn't sure this would hold the Quayloon, but because the roots of the Guardian continued to plunge far into the earth, I felt it might still have enough life to hold it. And for centuries, until last week, it has done so."

"So all we need to do is get the cabinet back, right? The one from my back room? Why didn't you say so? Why this long, drawn-out story?" Helen crossed her arms in front of her, huffing.

"Because just bringing the cabinet back here will probably not work. It's been separated from the life of the Guardian. It's no longer a part of it. I don't think that will work. I think we must bring it back, certainly, but we must try to locate another Guardian, a young one, and maybe somehow connect it to the cabinet that held the Quayloon for so many years. I have just about given up hope, though, because I have searched and searched the forest and have not located one. The Quayloon may have already won."

"A young one!" Helen jumped up from her chair, knocking it over again but ignoring it this time. "Flee, wait!" She yelled again. "I can't believe I didn't get the connection sooner. I think I may have *two* Guardians! Come on!" She ran toward the door and then outside. When she didn't follow her, she ran back inside and grabbed her hand, pulling her to the door. Flee floated behind her.

"See?! What are these? I found them a few years ago way out in the forest. They were so beautiful and so unique. I'd never seen anything like them, and they smelled like the wood in my house. In my house!"

Flee shimmered brightly in the sunlight, no longer solid. She floated around the little trees that were healthy and had already begun to grow tall and strong. Then other apparitions appeared around her, circling her, circling the trees. "Yes, yes. These are Guardians! I was so convinced there were no more that I couldn't see what was right before my eyes. I certainly never thought to look in a garden."

"They're really small, though. Can they hold the kwaloon?"

"They certainly can. And we won't even have to use the cabinet. The Guardians do not hold the Quayloon because of their size. I don't know how they hold it, but small ones can hold it as well as large ones. The only reason we relied on the Guardian used to construct your house was because it was the only one left, or at least that's what I thought. Apparently, even back then, there was one more Guardian deep in the forest where you found these trees, a Guardian that dropped at least two seeds, two seeds that will save all the lives supported by this forest and beyond."

Flee then turned to Helen and pointed toward the other end of the garden where a bench sat. "Please go there and sit so you will be safe, and don't come near until I call you."

Helen walked to the bench and sat as she was directed. She watched while Flee gathered the Folk around the two Guardians standing tall in the garden. They seemed to grow immense, and bright light and an eerie sort of music rose and encircled them. Then they all disappeared: the Guardians, the Folk, Flee, the light. All that remained was the sound of the music, strange, spectral music, floating up into the air. Then an agonizing shriek pierced the music, and a thick, black presence appeared where Flee and the trees had been just moments before, a putrid smell filling the air. Suddenly, blinding light illuminated the entire forest, and Helen was thrown to the ground, unconscious.

It was dark when she awoke, now lying on the bench. As her eyes adjusted, she saw that Flee was gone, the Folk were gone, and that awful black presence was gone. The two Guardian trees stood as if nothing had happened. She looked at them with pride and promised herself she would always care for those trees as long as she was alive. She got up and walked into the house.

"Flee, you in here?" When she got no answer, she walked into the newly renovated room, a room big enough to hold a rather large, battered old cabinet that she would retrieve tomorrow. She then walked back to the kitchen, sat down, and reached for her laptop. As Flee, unseen, watched over her, Helen typed on her laptop, "Once upon a time in a house in the woods…."

A MATTER OF FAITH
By Ross M Kitson

1.

What is faith? Is it the blind man driven by others, each step guided by trust? Or is it the blind man who follows his heart, his instinct, knowing the next step may take him along an erroneous path—yet realising it is the journey, and the destination, that is the true act of the faithful? When we strive to serve the cause of the just, of the Lord who is Mortis above, surely it is the achievement of the act that justifies the acts we must partake in? And the acts...are they not a means to an end?

Forgive my sins; forgive my actions, and my omissions. For in slaying the greater evil, in saving souls tainted by the Pale, I have consorted with witches. A witch. A changeling.

Oh Mortis above, the one true god whose fiery orb cleanses all that is sorcerous, hear my confession.

Hear it and forgive.

2.

The staghorn tore through the chainmail hauberk and emerged in a shower of crimson droplets. A look of confusion distorted Vordin's face as his hands felt the jagged tips of his death.

"Vordin! By Mortis...No!"

Sir Mortimer's scream seemed muffled in the density of the unnatural forest. His lunge towards the stag felt slurred, as if he moved through the depths of ocean. The monstrous creature reared its head, and Vordin's corpse slid down the horn and slumped across its back.

In the emerald dinge of the forest, Mortimer could see the horns glittering with metallic lustre. He faltered in horror as the stag tossed Vordin to the side and lowered its iron antlers in readiness.

What blasphemy is this? What fell stain on nature's beauty? His eyes met those of the stag.

Such ruminations dissipated like morning mist as the fiery surge of combat ignited his veins. The stag charged and he twisted, spinning across its flank and slicing with sword and dagger. The edge of his ornate longsword clattered off the metal antlers, but the dagger plunged deep into the creature's thorax. It shimmered with sacred power, and the stag stumbled, blood gushing from the deep rent.

"Suffer not the demon to walk the lands of the Father," he said. "The null-blade fears no witchery."

As the stag turned he hacked down with his sword and it bit deep into the creature's back. Evidently not all of it was bolstered by iron. Viscera writhed forth and a second blow cleaved the stag in twain.

Sir Mortimer staggered back against a tree, sweat running inside his plate armour.

The green glow that permeated the forest reflected off Vordin's dull stare. The purple and gold of his Godsarm tunic was soaked with blood and twisted into the chainmail and the gaping hole in his chest. "My dear friend, what has Lurfir and the Inquisition got us into?" he said. Mortimer began to sheath his sword when a voice made him jump.

"Watch out, you idiot."

A woman's voice..?

A furry shape the size of a small pony slammed into him. The impact sent him hurtling down the slope towards a stream. He was barely aware of the metallic tusks screeching across his breastplate. The looming trunks of the oaks and elms pivoted and spun in a jade kaleidoscope across his vision as he clutched for something solid to slow his descent. With a force that smashed the air from his lungs, he landed on the banks of the stream, feeling as if a huge claw squeezed his chest, mocking his laborious attempts at breathing.

Dear God. I need to get up. It will kill me.

On the edge of his fuzzy vision, he could see a huge boar scrabbling down the slope, drool swinging in glistening tendrils from its panting maw. Its tusks were iron and its massive skull misshapen and dented, like an old cauldron.

The thick mud of the banking clutched greedily at his limbs as he tried to stand. His armour, whilst a boon on the battlefield astride a thundering charger, was not well-suited to a melee in ankle deep mud. He raised his sword, numbly aware that his left hand no longer wielded the null-blade.

The boar leapt with terrifying momentum. Mortimer steeled himself for death.

A tan shape hurtled past him and into the boar. Claws and teeth gouged crimson furrows across the filthy pelt. Mortimer dropped, jabbing his sword upwards, but the edge caught the boar's skull with a clang of steel. The sword spun away and Mortimer overbalanced, searing pain ripping across his ankle as he tumbled into the stream.

Water filled his vision and his mouth, and he scrambled to gain his footing again as the current dragged at his armoured body. Raw fear at drowning overcame every other instinct, and he clutched at the slithering mud of the banks to get free of the waters.

The boar splashed in the stream, attempting to gore a large mountain lion which darted around. Claws ripped chunks from the boar, teeth shredding fur and flesh down to the bone. With horror, Mortimer saw the shine of metal plating the bones of the boar.

How can the lion defeat such a demon?

As if in reply to his thoughts, the lion sprang into the air. Its flesh rippled and warped, like a wax candle held close to a fire. In two heartbeats it had become a chestnut mare which plummeted onto the boar, a ton of weight driving the creature into the waters. The boar thrashed and struggled, but the horse trampled and stomped, keeping it under the water. Slowly the desperate protestations ebbed and the boar drowned.

Sir Mortimer clambered from the stream and stumbled up the slope to regain his sword. Mud smeared his armour and clogged his once neat hair and beard. His wavering hands grasped the sword as the horse stepped from the stream.

"Reveal your true self, changeling," he said. "In the name of the Father, Mortis, whose flaming eye sees all that's pure and virtuous, and…"

"If wars were won with words, you Goldorians would have an empire from the shores of Eeria to Shorvor."

The horse had transformed once more. In its stead stood a woman with short curly hair, as chestnut as the mane of the horse she had been but moments before. Her naked body was covered in swirling tattoos, spreading like fine black ivy from intricate designs on her ample bosom.

With herculean effort Sir Mortimer closed his gawping mouth and hefted his sword. The woman's eyes glittered dangerously as she prowled along the muddy bank.

"What business has the Goldorian Inquisition in the forests at the fringes of their nation? What do you know about these abominations?" the woman asked.

"Witch! We shall not suffer thee to live."

Mortimer lunged forwards, sword arcing towards the woman. She moved with the grace of a cat, darting to the side and scooping a sword from the ferns of the slope. The knight's slash cut only thin air, and he recovered to thrust again at the woman. With a grunt she parried the attack and weaved to the side. Mortimer's armour slowed his response, and a brisk pain burned his ankle. He was ill prepared for the swiftness of her blow to his flank. The force overbalanced him, and he tumbled once again into the water.

As he tried to rise, he felt the keen edge of the sword against his throat. He froze.

"Now firstly, I'm not a witch. I'm a druid—an Artorian druid, and you'll be more than aware that we were once a people who spawned an empire renowned for lack of compromise and violent solutions to any dispute. So I'll give you five seconds before I send your pious arse to the arms of your deity along with your unfortunate companion."

"Witch, I'll not…"

"Five…"

"Fear death…"

"Four, three…"

"Or tell you…"

"Two, one…"

"Wait!"

Blood trickled from the tip of the sword. Mortimer dare not swallow as he stared into the druid's green eyes. They were the eyes of a predator.

"Wait. We were sent here, Vordin and I, by the Archbishop. We are the Inquisition, and..."

"Where's the third member, the assassin?"

"Lurfir, of the Sacred Knife, remains in Parok. His role was reconnaissance."

"Hmm? Well, you need to get your money back there, Sir..?"

"Mortimer. Sir Pergin Mortimer, of Valikshall."

The druid eased the pressure of the blade and stepped back. "Go on."

"The peasants of the lands bordering the forest had gone to the Archbishop with claims of demonic animals found floating in the river that runs through the woodlands. Terrible beasts, a blasphemous distortion of the natural order..."

"More likely to be blasphemous to me as a druid, I'd warrant," she said.

Mortimer shrugged. The druids were followers of Nolir, the goddess of earth and patron to South Artoria, a nation on the far side of the Khullian Mountains.

"All sorcery is heresy," Mortimer stated. "These animals were abominations—distorted bodies with metal parts jutting from their torsos and congealed ore running from their mouths. The clergy were hard-pressed to purify and bless the waters for the peasants."

"I'm certain the whole place is still cursed, blessings aside," the druid said. "I can feel the pain of the Goddess, the wound in her body. There is a malignancy here—a sickness of the earth, and I have come to excise it."

"No—that's *my* quest, my test..."

The druid stared at Mortimer and erupted into laughter. He flushed a ruddy crimson.

"Your test? So you've only just been drafted into the Inquisition? Well, lucky you. I'd say it's not going too well at present. Why not work with me towards our common goal?"

The look of incredulity on Mortimer's face brought another burst of laughter from the druid. She rested the sword on her shoulder as he climbed from the stream. He tried not to stare at her voluptuous figure.

"Absolutely not. 'Parley not with the witch, for the tongue of sorcery is forked.' I cannot trust you, will not trust you."

"Well, having saved your life and now spared it, I'd guess it becomes a matter of honour versus faith. Which one trumps the other?"

A knot of indecision gripped Mortimer's belly. This was the trickery of the deviant, the glib words of a foreign mage. Yet she had had no need to save him, and druids were not true mages, true witches—they were priestesses of the earth goddess, with a source of magical power shrouded in mystery and contradiction.

His eyes darted around for his null-blade. Surely if he held its sacred metal, then he would be certain.

The druid had retrieved a small bag which she strapped around her bare back. She tossed the sword into the stream, then met Mortimer's gaze.

"Faith," he replied.

She shrugged. "Then keep out of my way, knight. And just so you don't get any stupid ideas…"

The druid held up the ornate null-blade and then dropped it into her bag. Its pommel, the shape of a lion's head, shimmered with power.

"Now as I recall, the blade only counteracts sorcery whilst grasped," she said. So it's best tucked away from your sweaty palm, and my chest."

Her body warped and writhed until it was replaced by the muscular shape of a lion. With a low growl, the cat sprang up the slope and into the density of the forest. Mortimer watched with a mixture of awe and disgust.

A voice echoed around the trees. "And if you change your mind, just call out my name and I'll hear."

"Your…name…?"

"Marthir. My name is Marthir."

3.

Thick oily smoke spiralled towards the canopy as Mortimer watched Vordin's corpse burn. He had had no choice. Although traditionally Goldorians buried their dead amidst prayers and reflections on the life of the deceased, such luxury was not available in the depths of the forest. And he shuddered to think of the desecration that the demonic animals would enact upon the corpse.

"Mortis embrace your soul," Mortimer said. "You died with bravery, cleansing the deviant."

The words congealed in his mouth. Vordin had been a difficult companion, evidently irked by Mortimer's inexperience and by the assignment so far from the purple stone of Goldoria City.

Yet he died without a stain on his immortal soul, without consorting with the impure.

He couldn't shake the image of Marthir's tattooed body from his mind. It beguiled and disgusted him in equal measures, drawing upon instincts long since battered into the recesses of his mind by the harsh training of a knight. The transient pleasures of the flesh required for procreation of heirs were forbidden until a knight ceased active service.

Is she part of the test? He considered it as he hobbled away from the funeral pyre. His oil bottle was empty, and he tossed away his unlit torches from his pack.

Don't be an idiot, Mort. Those of the Sacred Knife are many things, do many questionable acts, but contriving to use a witch as part of a test...that's surely beyond them.

He recalled the dark features of Lurfir shrouded in the gloom at the fringes of the Archbishop's chambers. It had been the holy assassin who had sought out Sir Mortimer the summer just past and who had overseen the training in inquisitorial methods required for the elite brotherhood.

And the druid, is she truly a witch? To others she would be a cleric, a priestess, with powers bestowed by her goddess. She did not have the foul gem of power in her chest like the wizards of the elemental orders nor the command of the mind that a Wild Mage would have.

No, sorcery is sorcery irrespective of source. Suffer not a witch to live. That is the creed of Mortis. Only in the fire of a sacred pyre may she gain salvation and forgiveness.

Yet she suffered me to live. Saved me, and then spared me, knowing I would despise her for it. Is this test in truth from the Father above, a trial of my honour versus my faith?

And the druid had taken his null-blade. Crafted from an alloy of magnate and steel, the mixture of God-silver and mortal metal allowed the blade to retain a wondrous blessing. The null-blade could repel and annul sorcery, offering protection to the knights in their battles against warlocks and demons.

She knows of its power and how that might is tapped. Who is she to be aware of our knighthood and my nation of Goldoria?

A howl shattered his train of thought. The wolves' call was answered thrice over. There were hunters in the woodlands, and Mortimer knew with sudden certainty that they would scarcely be normal wolves. He broke into a run and then stumbled as his ankle locked in pain.

"By the gods, I'm easy prey, hobbled as I am."

Dusk was approaching, and the scanty light of the forest was leaching away into gloom. The contorted trees threw complicated shadows all around making progress treacherous, and doubly so with an injured ankle. His filthy plate armour weighed heavily on his broad frame, the intricate embossed magnate barely discernible beneath the mud. Brambles scratches at his cheeks, drawing fine stinging tracts of red.

Another howl, and a jolt of primordial terror shook his chest. Praying for resolve, Mortimer pushed onwards into the forest, hacking weeds and ferns from his path. He had no oil, no torches. Within the hour he would be staggering blind through the forest with no idea what he sought.

The druid knows what she seeks—what we both seek.

The graveyard glow of three moons transiently lit the forest ahead as a stormy cloud moved in the sky. In the distance, atop the slopes where the forest rose into the foothills of the North Khullian Mountains, he could see a pack of wolves. Their eyes glowed a demonic green, and the silver of the Eerian moon glittered on the metal of their limbs and jaws.

Mortimer cowered behind a tree, convinced the same moonlight would reflect off his armour and sword. *Four of them—I would have no chance, as good a swordsman as I am.*

Not as swift as the druid though. How can she fight so adeptly?

Is it heresy to think of her? Is it blasphemy to consider an alliance? A temporary measure, to fulfil my mission. What value is my training, my devoted swordarm, if I die choking in filth as wolves tear apart my flesh? Surely this is the only path I can take?

The wolves had moved into the murk of the forest. Mortimer licked the sweat from his moustache and pressed his forehead wearily against the pommel of his sword.

"Mortis forgive me. Marthir."

A lion padded from the darkness. It had been so close it could have pounced and killed him before he'd be able to raise a sword. Its green eyes regarded him coldly.

"Marthir, damn you," Mortimer said. "I need your help."

The lion's fur flowed and warped into human shape. Marthir leaned back against a tree, her nudity illuminated by the moons. Mortimer blushed and looked away.

"You'll need to get used to my aversion to clothes," Marthir said. "In the middle of a battle, I don't want you distracted by my breasts."

"Mortis's sake, woman. In the name of decency…"

"Oh, hush your Goldorian prudery. Those four wolves will catch your scent any moment and not cease until they're feasting on your devout entrails."

"I…I can't run quickly. My ankle turned when I fell into the stream."

Marthir frowned and approached Mortimer. She crouched and tugged loose some rubbery herbs from the base of a tree. Her nose wrinkled as she smelled the leaves.

"Hold still."

The druid began smearing the sap from the leaves over Mortimer's armour. The stink made his eyes blur with tears. Even Marthir was balked at the odour.

Up close the druid's tattoos seemed almost alive, appearing to ripple under the tan of her smooth skin. Runes and swirls were knitted together in a macabre intricate design. Marthir caught Mortimer's gaze, and she hesitated. Her hand indicated the densest area of tattoo on her left breast.

"The heart sign, the root of the designs of Nolir. Painted on by my mentor, Derusia. It's like the keystone in my own personal temple."

"The runes, the patterns…are they…spells?"

"Ha! No, no. They're scripture. Carried on our skin in a manner that may only be taken by death."

"Your…scripture? Dear Mortis…"

"You can read it later," Marthir said. "Now I've pasted you in Pale Spit—it's not so poisonous, although it stinks like a Pyrian privy in the height of summer."

"I'll never get the stench from my armour."

"At least you'll be alive to try. Now follow this trail along the valley, and you should find the old trade road close to the river. The maps I read suggest it used to run into the hills. If there's shelter it'll be along that way—and the higher grounds were where the stags and boars tend to roam."

"Shelter?"

"There used to be miners in the foothills, so there must be some old places up that way. Even a ruin's better than being out in the open when the storm comes."

Mortimer glanced at the imposing sky. The moons had eased behind a malignant cloud. The air had a dreadful stillness.

"Go. I'll lead them astray with a far more enticing scent," Marthir said. "I'll catch you up."

"And my null-blade?"

"Stays with me," Marthir said. "One thing at a time, eh?"

And with that she transformed into a lion and prowled away.

4.

The rain hammered down on the overgrown road, turning the baked mud slick and brown. The sharp pain in Mortimer's ankle had faded into continual gnawing agony. He staggered, the incessant rain forcing him towards the mud. Water sloshed into his boots, chilling needles working their deadly way through his bones.

This is no way for a knight to die, wallowing like a swine in the dirt.

A surge of pride lifted him like an ethereal hand. Step by painful step, he regained his feet and resumed his journey along the road. Would the druid rejoin him, or had she fallen to the demonic wolves? Alone they were vulnerable—together claw, hoof and sword could prevail.

Skeletal remains of habitation materialised through the curtains of rain. Cadaverous holes in the moss-daubed stone hinted at dark secrets best left alone. Instinct drove Mortimer's legs past the potential shelters towards something more substantial.

"Sir?"

In a smooth reflex motion, Mortimer's sword was in his hand. A terrified child was on the road before him. His threadbare clothes were pasted to his minute frame, and his sandy hair hung in thick tendrils over his shoulders.

"Boy? What in the Lord Above's name are you doing here in the forest?"

"Begging your pardon, m'lord. I live here."

"In the ruins?"

The boy shook his head. "N-no, m'lord. In my house, with my ma."

Slowly Mortimer lowered his sword. The boy stepped forward and regarded him. His eyes were dark blue, as deep and mysterious as the ocean at night.

"Then take me to your hearth, lad. It is the right of the knighthood to claim Lord's Shelter."

The boy bowed. "As you say, sir. My ma will be honoured. But we must make haste, for dark creatures curse the night."

Mortimer struggled to keep up with the boy's nimble pace. At times the child seemed to merge with dark haze of the storm wracked forest, such that Mortimer wondered if he was some spirit or revenant sent to tempt him off the path.

Marthir has done that already…

The notion evaporated as a house appeared from the rain at the fringe of the road. Its dark stone structure stood in contrast to the lush woodland around it, as stark as a blood stain on white linen. Brass sconces framed the heavy oak door, giving a fleeting appearance of a leering mouth. Ivy wove across the exterior, intertwined and convoluted like a druid's tattoos.

A woman opened the door and cupped her hands to call. "Aron? Come inside, my love. Come…"

She faltered as she saw Mortimer. Her gaze rested on his sword.

"S-sir, spare us," she begged. "I beseech you, no harm was meant."

"Goodwife, spare me words that are wasted on the winds," Mortimer said. "I have hunger and thirst enough to humble an army and demand the tithe of shelter and food."

"No need to demand, m'lord," Aron said. "Tis freely offered."

Ignoring the mother's hiss, Mortimer regarded the lad and his sincere stare. He nodded gruffly. "Your sharp tongue does me shame, boy. I'm tired and in pain, soaked to the skin and covered in a crippling stench. Yet, I offer apology—though my demands remain the same. A Lord's Shelter."

The woman seemed to shudder as Mortimer and Aron entered the warm interior of the house. A transient shame at the fear he must be causing the peasant girl was quickly overcome by his need for rest and cleanliness. He sheathed his sword and slumped at the kitchen table, sleep overpowering him as surely as Marthir had those hours before.

5.

The boy had brought several kettles of scalding water to warm the chill of the ceramic bath. It took almost an hour for Mortimer to scrub the grime of the forest away. At his familial estate in mid-Goldoria, there were servants to perform such functions, and self-care came with difficulty to the knight. His ankle was a ruddy swollen purple.

An old tunic had been laid out on the bed. Its threads were worn with time, and the style one Mortimer remembered from his youth. He donned it and pulled the belt tight around his muscular waist. It took a minute to secure his sword, and he then exited the guest room into the hallway.

The interior of the house was well maintained. It had evidently once been the residence of someone with status as the wood and stone was of good quality and engraved with care. Despite its cleanliness there was an earthy smell to the place, as if it were buried in the soil of the forest. And there was something else—a weight to the place, a density in the air.

Mortimer spotted his armour in the sitting room. The boy had been cleaning it diligently whilst Mortimer bathed, and it glittered in the light from the hearth. The plates were set separately from the chainmail hauberk which had proven trickier to clean.

"M'lord?"

Mortimer started, and then turned to scowl at the boy. "Creeping about the house like that! Secrets are the nectar of the heretic. Has your mother prepared food?"

"Almost, sir. There's something else…someone else who has arrived. At the door."

His heart sinking, Mortimer asked, "And…how is she attired?"

The boy smiled strangely. "Why, in a robe, sir."

Wearing a confused expression, Mortimer followed the boy to the porch. The boy's mother was standing with her arms folded, blocking the entrance, and on the far side of her Mortimer saw Marthir. She wore a plain dark brown robe that covered her tanned legs and arms down to mid-forearm. Her small pack was on her shoulder.

"We've no time for foreigners here," the mother said. "Be off with you."

"You've enough time to have learned Imperial, ma'am," Marthir replied. "Unusual for a forester on the edge of Goldoria."

"Ma was a trader for the woodsmen before Da passed," Aron said. His observation earned him a glare from his mother.

"Well, I'm sorry for your loss, but I'd welcome the chance to join my companion, Sir Mortimer."

Aron and his mother turned and looked at Mortimer. He cleared his throat. "Ah, umm, yes…we are acquainted. Lady Marthir is a…a…pilgrim…um, assisting me. In my quest."

"A pilgrim? M'lord, she…her marks…"

The robe barely covered the tattoos on Marthir's arms. The druid's eyes flared with feral anger. Before Mortimer could answer, the boy placed a hand on his mother's chest.

"We will let her in now."

The mother stared at Aron and then nodded slowly, before stepping aside. Marthir smiled and bowed to Aron, then entered the house.

"Sir Mortimer, you've scrubbed up well," Marthir said gaily. She strode past the three and into the kitchen, keeping her pack close to her side.

Mortimer caught her up. "I could say the same," he hissed. "Where did you get the clothes, and why didn't you wear them before, in the woods?"

"From my pack, of course," Marthir said. "And most men don't object when I don't wear them."

His cheeks burning as hot as the stove, Mortimer sat at the kitchen table. Aron and his mother entered, and silently she began to serve the mushroom stew from the pot.

"My apology for being so rude before," Marthir said to the mother. "I'm Marthir of Keresh in Artoria. And your name?"

"Tara," the mother said, avoiding Marthir's gaze.

A silence seeped across the table as the four began to eat. Mortimer swiftly finished the bowl and watched as Tara served him a second.

"What a curious house you have," Marthir said. "Where all the others are ruins, this has stood the test of time admirably."

"We stayed here with Da when the others all left," Aron said.

"I see. Yet it's still so…preserved, as if the forest nurtures it," Marthir said.

"We are happy here. Our lives are simple," Tara said. "We have all we need."

Aron shrugged. "I dream of leaving the woods, going to the wondrous sights that the Father Above has inspired. I have so much to offer, don't I, Mother?"

Tara's hands were white with tension on her spoon. "Yes, Aron, you do."

"The boy has lofty ambitions," Mortimer said chewing a mushroom. "The industrial marvels of Goldoria City have to be seen to be believed. The great funicular that ascends the pinnacle; the huge hoists and cranes at the docks in the Merchant Quarter; the clockmakers of the Old Quarter…"

Marthir reached into her pack and drew forth a silver timepiece. She twirled it around her hand. Mortimer's eyes widened. Aron looked with curiosity.

"Where did you..?"

"My husband is Goldorian and inherited a love of timepieces from his father. It always fascinated me as an Artorian, the Goldorian affection for technology."

"Born from our nation's hatred of sorcery," Mortimer said. "As I'm sure you know. After all, if there's no wizard to raise the mighty stones to build your city, then where else can you turn?"

"One day it'll all be gone," Aron said.

Marthir looked at the boy in confusion. "What will?"

"The greenery, the trees, the fields. Iron and steel will trample over it all, and fire will scour the lush woodlands until all is hard and cold and grey."

Exchanging a concerned look with Mortimer, Marthir leaned towards the boy. "How long has the forest been cursed?"

"That's why they left, isn't it, Ma?" Aron said. "When those miners all died."

Tara shook, tears running down her face.

"Ma! Tell them!"

Her voice tremulous, Tara stared at her bowl of stew as she spoke. "We thought it a plague at first. One of the woodsmen had found them all dead, to a man. But their bodies, when we brought them down from the hills to bury them…they were…cursed.

"Parts of them were hard, tougher, not the gripe that death brings, but…solid. My husband, Lyrik, he scraped the skin away from one of them. The muscle had become metal, turned to iron.

"The other woodsmen—they burned the bodies, to dispel the witchcraft, and then they went. All of them, left to march to Parok."

Mortimer was smoothing his moustache in thought. Marthir placed her hand atop Tara's to steady it.

"And why did you stay?"

"Aron…Aron went to the mines—a boy's curiosity. Lyrik had to go and bring him back, and that night…when they got back…"

"Mother…" Aron began.

"The wolves came…they took Lyrik from the road, and…we never saw him again."

"Yet you escaped them?" Marthir asked Aron.

Aron nodded. He stared at his mother with an inscrutable expression.

"And you're still here?" Marthir asked.

"Obviously." Tara stood abruptly and began cleaning the bowls away. Tears jerked her slim body as she busied around the kitchen.

"The mine. What was there, boy?" Mortimer asked.

Aron shuddered. "Nothing to see, sir. Just a feeling, like a presence...a very old, very dark presence."

"Then that is where we shall seek the root of this evil," Mortimer said, slamming his hand on the table. "How far is the mine?"

"Three miles, sir. But the rain will have made it muddy—your plate armour will be too heavy for you to get there in."

"The knight is more than his plate armour!" Mortimer said. "I shall travel with but a chainmail hauberk, Lady Marthir. Virtually bare, by knightly standards."

Marthir tugged playfully at the neckline of her robe and winked at Mortimer. The knight scowled and attempted to expunge every impure thought from his mind.

6.

The density of the forest lightened as the ground got higher at the fringes of the foothills. The bulbous contorted roots of the trees retreated from the edges of the path, allowing Marthir's hooves to break into a canter. Mortimer held tightly to her neck, unused to riding without bridle and tack.

In the distance the rocks of the foothills marked the entrance to the copper mines. Marthir slowed to a trot and then halted. Mortimer dismounted, cursing as his ankle buckled.

Marthir transformed from equine to human form and crouched by the knight whilst he sat against a tree.

"Let me take a look at the ankle."

"And work your witchery upon it? I think not."

"It needs a decent strapping, and no 'witchery,' I promise."

With the air of a sulky child, Mortimer gingerly removed his boot. With expert fingers, Marthir examined the swelling.

"It's a bad sprain. Bones are fine enough. I'll strap it to ease the pain."

"Unusual for a druid to know such things," Mortimer observed as Marthir began wrapping cloth tightly. Their packs were replenished with vials of oil, a rope, dried food, and water from Tara's house. In Marthir's small pack he could discern the hilt of the null-blade.

"I was an Artorian tracker before I got the calling to the goddess," Marthir said.

That explains her skill with a sword and her healing knowledge, Mortimer thought. Trackers were Artorian scouts, trained in South Artoria to spy upon their Northern Artorian enemies. Their elite status was well earned.

"I'll admit the track wasn't as muddy as I was expecting," Mortimer said. "I think I could have brought my plate armour after all."

"Aron was too busy polishing it," Marthir said. "Probably plans to sell it if we end up as wolf fodder."

Mortimer snorted and looked down the track to the mines. "A strange child to be sure. And the mother. I've no children of my own, but if I had lost my husband to demonic wolves, I'd hardly be letting my son wander the forest on his own."

"And the rest of their community…" Marthir began.

"Indeed. The foresters never made it to Parok. There was no record of any such arrival."

"The forest evidently doesn't relinquish its own so readily," Marthir said. "And I see what you mean about Aron and Tara."

"Yes. Odd. He said all the right things, but his demeanour was most…atypical. Tara seemed almost to be…fearful when we were there."

"Well, the answers won't be found taking a nap in the dirt," Marthir said. "How's the ankle feel?"

With a wince, Mortimer got to his feet. "You have my gratitude again."

"I'm accumulating favours," Marthir said. "Sure you'll pay them back."

With a nod, Sir Mortimer limped down the track as it wove up into the hills.

7.

The rocky face of the minehead emerged from the dense foliage as Marthir and Mortimer reached the end of the track. Several wagons had rotted into the carpet of ferns, like ships floundering in an emerald sea. The remnants of a track for the mine ran from the wagons to a jagged hole in the rocks. There was a palpable tension in the air, as if a storm were about to break.

Mortimer drew his sword and approached the hole that marked the entrance. Out of the corner of his vision, he could see Marthir hesitate, rubbing her forehead in discomfort.

"Are you..?"

"I'm fine. The earth power is distorted here, diseased."

"Let us be quick then," Mortimer said. He hobbled through the hole and into a thin high-roofed cave. He paused to light his lantern. Marthir brushed past him, her bare feet soundless on the rock floor.

Without words the duo advanced through the cave and into a corridor hewn into the rock. Heavy wooden beams braced the walls and ceiling. The air was as chill and stagnant as a grave. The passage descended at a steep angle into the roots of the hill. In time it broadened into a larger chamber from which a dozen exits departed. The nearest to the right was little more than a crevice opening out onto a dark precipice.

"This opening is fresher than those others," Marthir said. "You can see the tool marks far easier."

The pair slipped through the gap and to the edge of the precipice. The gloom was so marked it made Mortimer's eyes ache. He scooped a stone and tossed it over the edge. It took several seconds before he heard the clatter.

"A good hundred feet," Mortimer said.

With a sigh, Marthir tugged loose a coil of rope. "I'll lower you down."

"Surely I'm a better anchor with my weight," Mortimer said. His words faltered as Marthir turned into a horse. With a shrug, he looped the rope around her back and belly, the other end around his waist, and then clambered over the edge.

The amber pool of the lantern struggled to cut through the viscous gloom. Within a minute, Mortimer felt somehow removed from the world. In his gut arose a nagging terror that some sorcerous trick would leave him eternally descending, or worse, without enough rope to reach the bottom.

The rock was tricky to climb, more so for him wearing chainmail. The rope remained taut around him. Then abruptly the rope jerked on his chest.

There's no more, he thought. *I should be at the bottom now. It's a trick.*

Terror washed over him, and the darkness clawed at the edges of his lantern light. Any second now the druid witch would cut the rope and he would tumble to his death, lost forever in an ebony tomb. He began to scrabble at the rock, seeking a decent handhold in anticipation of the rope falling past him.

The rope slackened transiently then became taut once more.

"What...are you...playing at?" Marthir's voice echoed from above.

She's become human again, Mortimer thought. *To toss the...*

"Stop messing around," she said. "The bottom can only be ten feet off. I'll lower you down as best I can."

"How do you...?"

"I used to...be a bloody tracker. Now shut up, this rope is killing my arms."

His feet probing below, Mortimer climbed further down. After another ten feet, he still hadn't found the bottom of the cliff.

"Loosen the rope," Marthir called. "You need the extra length."

Mortimer pressed his face against the cool rock. He felt sick with fright.

"Trust me. Have faith."

The knight looked down into the depths of uncertainty. Trust...a druid? Was this act of faith truly a test from the gods?

Have faith.

He loosened the rope and gripped the free end. His boots skidded down the rock face.

And found the base of the cliff.

8.

The area at the base of the cliff was the size of a large room and hewn from the rock of the hill. Faint streaks of copper in the stone gave it an almost rusted quality. Mortimer could discern an order to the area, distinct remnants of columns running in two rows to a crumbled square plinth. The place stank of evil magic, a nauseating, sweet stench that cloyed at the senses.

"You all right, Mortimer?"

With a flash of guilt, Mortimer realised he'd been silent for a minute.

"I'm fine. It seems to be some kind of ruined shrine."

"To?"

The columns were worn smooth by the caress of the ages, but carvings were discernible on the plinth. Mortimer steeled himself and approached. Etched into the stone was a figure with a humanoid torso but a terrible fly's head.

"Sugox—demon duke of disease and plague."

A square section of the central plinth had been removed, and Mortimer could see a faint purple aura around the edges. His gaze drifted to the far side of the plinth, and he saw a black shape, like a small cloak laid across the dark rock. Mortimer brought his lantern closer and then recoiled as the cloak began to ripple.

"Revered Mortis, flies…"

A cloud of flies erupted from the plinth and swirled like a teeming vapour around Mortimer. He fell to his knees, covering his mouth and nose as they struck him, the buzzing mass crawling over his exposed skin.

Reclaim calm. All evil may be conquered, all sorcery purified.

His hands grasped the oil in his pack. He shattered the vial on the ground and then threw his lantern onto the spreading pool. There was a burst of flames and a whoosh of raw heat. Dense smoke poured from the flames, and Mortimer held his breath and stood in the torrent of smoke.

The flies dispersed in the smoke, some weaving upwards into the darkness, others dropping to the ground and crisping in the burning oil. The area around Mortimer was illuminated brightly by the conflagration, and covering his mouth from the fumes, he quickly surveyed the aspects previously concealed. His gaze fell upon the plinth, and he saw tattered remains of cloth with ivory fragments jutting forth.

A skeleton. A child's skeleton.

Terrible realisation washed over him. "Marthir," he shouted. "I need to come back up. Now."

The end of the rope dangled, and he jumped and held onto it. There was a grunt from above. The druid was clearly taking all the weight in her human form. Mortimer ascended the rock face through clouds of oily smoke, his mind racing as his hands scraped at the rocks.

He achieved the edge of the precipice to find Marthir bolstered against two heavy rocks. Sweat ran in rivulets down her tattooed body.

"You could have ditched the bloody mail hauberk," Marthir said through gritted teeth.

"No. No, don't you see?" Mortimer said. "That's what he wanted!"

"Who? What are you rambling about?"

"Aron. The boy. Except he's not a boy. What was Aron is at the bottom of the cliff—he must have fallen and struck the altar."

"Then the boy is…"

"A demon. We must return to the house, now. He has my magnate armour."

The pair sprinted down the passage, the pool of light from Marthir's lantern dancing across the rough walls. As they emerged into the entrance, they slowed their pace. A pack of four wolves approached, demonic eyes narrowed in hatred. The lantern light glittered off areas of metal fur and copper teeth.

In a blur of flesh, Marthir became a lion and sprang. Mortimer drew his sword and lunged at the nearest wolf. It darted to his side, its metal teeth seeking exposed flesh on his legs. He slashed downwards, but his blade clattered off the beast's metal neck. Its teeth snapped furiously against his mail hauberk as he retreated towards the passage, aware of a second wolf circling to his flank.

Marthir fought with astonishing speed, a flurry of tooth and claw. Yet the futility of the battle was apparent as the wolves' enhanced metallic bodies repelled attack after attack. The mutated beasts pushed them back into the narrow passage. The largest wolf lunged at Marthir, and she rolled back, flipping it up and over into the wooden braces of the passage with a splintering crash. Rocks rained around Mortimer's head as the strained beams cracked and gave way.

Rocks and dust cascaded as the passage collapsed.

9.

Mortimer emerged from fitful memories of dour priests and iron discipline into consciousness. Dense darkness surrounded him. He gingerly checked over his body, finding only scrapes and bruises. Above him he could feel rocks and a thick wooden beam bracing the collapsed ceiling. There was barely room to stand.

"Marthir?" he hissed. The air was choked with dust and already stale.

His shaking hands probed into the inky blackness and found warm bare flesh. They rested for a moment on the smooth contours of Marthir's hip. He gently shook her.

She awoke with a start, sitting up and smacking her head on the rocks. Curses were soon followed by sobs. Mortimer recoiled in confusion.

"Sweet Goddess, not this. Please, not this."

Revered Mortis, she is terrified. Of being buried.

Battering down his own fear, he grasped her trembling body. She pushed into him, seeking the solace of his muscular chest. He rested his face against her dust-clogged hair. There was a feral muskiness to her that raged through his senses. His lips moved past her ear and onto her face. She responded with a greedy kiss, chewing his lip, bringing the metallic taste of blood into his mouth.

Passion overwhelmed him, and he pressed against her naked form. Her hands tore open the straps on his hauberk, her nails raking over his exposed skin. He moaned in delight and at the release of his opened britches. In the darkness she moved over him with an undeniable force, her breasts pressing hard against him as her hands found his excitement.

Without words they became one, gasps and cries of long supressed desires echoing around the confines of their dusty tomb. With a cry bordering on pain, Mortimer jerked and then fell back spent. A beatific sense consumed him as he felt Marthir wrapped around him, and they lay for a time in an embrace.

"I don't imagine that's a usual inquisitorial method," Marthir said in time.

Mortimer felt sick at his weakness, yet warm and satisfied. The contradiction pinned him like a giant claw.

"I…dear Mortis, I took advantage…succumbed to temptation…I…"

"Did what men and woman have done since the gods created us. It's the creed of Nolir that passions of the flesh are to be welcomed. If we're to die together, then there are worse ways to spend our last hours, to use our last breaths of air."

The pair laid in silence for a time, both lost in rumination. In time, Marthir broke the quietness.

"The demon planned this, so as to get your magnate plate armour."

"Aye, presumably to graft onto more animals. The magnate alloy will make them near unstoppable."

"And the mother? She knows, you think?"

"Thinking on it, I can see her fear of him now. She knows. She's party to his blasphemy."

"Let's not cast the inquisitorial stones so readily—a mother's love can drive a woman to extreme measures."

Mortimer smoothed his moustache in the darkness. The air was thinning, yet he was certain he could feel a faint breeze against his arm.

"There was one more thing," he said. "A section of the altar was missing. There were no signs of it being forced out though."

"All academic if we're to be entombed here," Marthir said. The tremor had returned to her voice.

"I'm sure I can sense some air against me," Mortimer said. "So we must be close to an air pocket at least. Can you transform into something very small?"

Marthir pressed against him to try and feel the air flow. A tingle of excitement ran through him.

"No, each druid learns via…certain rituals…to be gifted with the form of a given animal. Though my brothers and sisters chose rabbits, stoats, and snakes I'm only gifted with horse and lion."

An ominous creak interrupted Marthir. Small rocks rained down upon the pair as the beam above them shifted. Mortimer stood and braced his back against the wood.

"If I can shift it, perhaps we can open a space for you to escape. The evil cannot flourish, cannot prevail."

Even with all this strength, the beam only shifted slightly and pain needled through his splinted ankle. Mortimer cursed and slumped next to Marthir. He supressed a sob of frustration.

"I'll do it."

"You? Well, I know you have determination and skill, my dear, but…"

"I'll transform into a horse and lift the beam as I do so."

A cold dread consumed Mortimer. "That would…well, it'll break your back. And if it fails, we'll both be crushed by the space you'll occupy."

Against his cheek, Mortimer felt Marthir's light touch. Her mouth was inches from his ear, her breath hot in his ear.

"I'd rather spend my last hours consummating our newfound allegiance, but this foul demon of the Pale is destroying the flesh of the goddess, corrupting her offspring. The peasants of Goldoria will be next, and despite what the clergy may deserve, the common folk need protection. One of us must escape to kill the demon."

"No. No, there must be some other way…"

Into Mortimer's palm, Marthir pressed the cool metal of the null-blade. It shimmered in the gloom, throwing a ghostly light on the small hollow they both lay in. Marthir's beautiful figure seemed to glow with its own primordial energy. For the first time, Mortimer did not avert his eyes but rather admired her. Gently Marthir kissed him and then stood, pressing her shoulders against the beam.

"Stick that in the demon's ribs, rather than mine?" she said.

Mortimer nodded and sheathed the blade. He checked his sword and then smiled to indicate his readiness.

With a ripple of magic, Marthir's flesh began to twist and warp. The tanned skin darkened to a chestnut hue and her hands became hoofs. As her face elongated into that of a horse, she screamed in pain as the beam creaked and lifted. Mortimer flattened himself down, aware of the escalating bulk above him. Rocks tumbled around as the stones shifted, and with a surge of hope he saw light stream through a gap in the hollow.

He scrambled forwards through the gap, jagged stone tearing at his exposed arms. Stone scraped along his chainmail, and for a terrifying moment he was snagged in the narrow tunnel. Raw panic throttled him as he could feel the tons of rock pressing from above.

Dear Mortis, I'll be crushed in an instant.

Marthir's scream had become a sickening whinny, and the noise jolted Mortimer from his fear. He shoved and the mail tugged loose. With a gasp he scrabbled along the tunnel, head battering against the descending rocks.

Daylight flooded his senses, and he crawled free onto the muddy grass of the hillside. Gulping the air greedily, he turned to look for something to support the diminishing tunnel, when it collapsed in a cloud of dust.

With a roar he flung himself against the uncaring rocks, his fingers scraping and scratching at the stones to try and free Marthir. In time his efforts ebbed and he slumped sobbing against the rubble.

She's dead. Crushed under the tons of rock—a fate that terrified her more than anything. Yet she sacrificed herself for her faith. For me.

Mortimer buried his face in his bloodied hands. He could still smell Marthir on him, still feel her touch.

I have lain with a woman, with a witch. Mortis forgive the pleasure I have indulged in.

Not a witch. A druid, a priestess, a foreigner, but not a witch.

Not a witch. A hero.

Slowly he stood and took a long deep breath. With one hand he drew his sword and with the other held his null-blade. There was no time for sorrow, no time for regret. There was only time for vengeance and justice.

He hobbled down the slope and back into the oppression of the forest.

10.

Night had invaded the forest by the time he reached the house. Yet the shadows seemed less intimidating with the penumbra of holy light that spilled from his null-blade. The pain in his ankle had become a distant memory as Mortimer's mind focused with the precision of a steel blade.

The foliage had fallen from the walls of the house, like a serpent shedding its skin. The stone pulsed with dark power, tiny lines of copper and silver working through the granite like metallic veins. The brass sconces undulated as if battling against the constraints of their form.

The house itself watches me, taunts me, goads me with what is contained in its evil innards.

"For Mortis. For Marthir," Mortimer muttered and pressed the flat of his sword against his forehead in salute. He strode to the door.

As he kicked it open, the brass sconces became long spikes and thrust towards him. He spun and parried, the null-blade crackling and cutting through the sorcerous metal with ease. In three steps he was in the small hallway, crouched in readiness. The walls hissed like a kettle on the stove. Mortimer felt tiny in contrast to the seething mass of stone and mortar and metal around him.

"Demon! By the Holy Father Mortis I call upon you to step forth," he called. "Your hour of reckoning is at hand."

Aron stepped into the hallway, his features twisted in a leer. In the adjacent kitchen, Mortimer could see Tara slumped, her body jerking with utter sorrow.

"You have more lives than a cat," Aron said. "Or at least a druid. Where is Nolir's little whore?"

"In the embrace of her deity, spawn of the Pale."

"Did she scream as she died? Did she beg…did she cry like a little child?"

"Silence. Your words are poison. Your deception is at an end. This shell you wear, this illusion of a child. What twisted cruelty..?"

"The mother. She begged and wailed at the broken body of her boy. On my altar, on my stone prison, the blood and the grief freed me. She brought me here, and I claimed this hovel as my own. Claimed it to regain my strength, to plan my conquest. A world of iron and steel, like my vast estates in the Pale. A fusion of mortal flesh and immortal unending metal."

"Even metal rusts," Mortimer hissed.

He lunged forward, slicing with his sword as he stabbed with the null-blade. Aron vaulted towards the ceiling, the attacks meeting only air. He scuttled along the walls like a spider. With a curse Mortimer hacked at him, chunks of stone and mortar showering around.

Aron flipped and landed in the kitchen. With his gesture all the utensils lifted and hurtled towards Mortimer, who dove behind the door frame, wincing as a knife jutted from the wood inches from his face.

He has control of all metals—he must be an iron demon.

The aura from the null-blade surrounded Mortimer and his sword as he broke cover and charged into the kitchen. Aron crouched on top of the kitchen table, laughing at the cries and misery of Tara.

"This ends now," Mortimer said. He swung his sword in a deadly arc towards Aron. The demon gestured at the blade, then looked in surprise as his sorcery failed to control Mortimer's sword.

Black blood spattered across the table and Tara's huddled form. The demon screamed as his hand spun across the kitchen, yet rolled away from the stab of the null-blade.

"Idiotic minion of Mortis," he spat as he danced away. "You think that little totem will save you?"

"Your sorcery may not affect all that I hold and wear, demon. Give my regards to Sugox on your way back into the Pale."

Emboldened by the black blood that coated the kitchen floor, Mortimer advanced with weapons readied.

"It is a shame that you're not wearing that splendid magnate armour then," Aron said.

A stream of magnate and steel burst through the kitchen wall and in an instant coalesced into a glittering fist. Mortimer barely had time to raise his sword as the fist slammed into him. The momentum carried him across the kitchen, and he smashed against the stone of the hearth. He felt his ribs splinter and blood in his mouth.

Taste of blood. Marthir biting as she kissed.

The kitchen was a blur of agony. The metal fist had turned into a claw that gripped his chest and pinned him to the stone. He was vaguely aware of Aron prowling towards him. His hands were limp and empty by his side.

Such pain. Can't breathe. All is cold, and hard, and metal. Where is the warmth? The heat of Marthir's passion. Hold onto that memory, draw strength. I will not beg.

"Don't die too quickly, knight. The souls of all those Dark Mages you sent to the Pale will want some recompense."

Two tendrils of metal grew from the huge claw and wormed towards Mortimer's eyes. Aron giggled, clutching the black stump of his wrist.

"Nice and slowly, through the windows of your soul, into that righteous brain…"

Mortis, grant me strength. Oh, gods…

The impact of the lion striking Aron was palpable from across the kitchen. He screamed as the lion's claws raked dark furrows in his small chest. Its jaws ripped a chunk of face away in a shower of black. Evil sorcery swirled around the demon and Marthir as they rolled across the floor.

The pressure in the magnate claw eased, and Mortimer stumbled free. He searched in desperation for his weapons. With horror he saw his sword lift from the floor and hurtle across the kitchen towards Marthir's back.

"No! Marthir!"

He leapt, but the pain in his chest diminished his strength. The sword plunged through his outstretched hand and into Marthir. His intervening hand had deflected the aim and the blade impaled her hip rather than her abdomen. Mortimer struck Marthir's leonine back, and they tumbled away into the kitchen table.

In a blur Marthir was human again. Blood soaked her tattooed flesh and she tugged at the sword that jutted through her hip and thigh. Mortimer moaned in pain as the metal grated against the bones in his palm.

"How…sweet."

Aron loomed above them. A flap of skin across his mouth hung like the peel of a rotten fruit. Black demon blood dripped onto the stones at his feet. It smoked with malignant power. The column of magnate and steel rose behind him, deadly blades emerging like shoots from a plant. The house seemed to pulse in excitement at what it was about to witness.

"Now let's end this quickly. Mother and I have things to attend to."

The column arched over him. Mortimer pulled Marthir close.

"You are not my son."

Tara drove the null-blade deep into the demon's heart. The ruin of its face stared at astonishment as she twisted it around and around. Black blood ran down her front as the demon crumpled.

With a cry of pain, Mortimer pulled Marthir to the side as the column of metal toppled. As they righted themselves, he saw in horror it had fallen upon Tara and Aron.

"Thank Nolir that's over," Marthir said through gritted teeth. "Now..."

"*Over?*" an ethereal voice said. "*Oh, little druid. You have no idea...*"

Dark sorcery swirled through the air of the house. The stones ground and scraped as the structure seemed to take a deep mocking breath. The metal of pots and pans and knives and forks flowed like mercury across the floor and joined with streams of metal entering from the other rooms.

"*I am a demon of the Pale, fifth consort to Sugox, honoured by the maggots of rust writhing in my festering womb. Destroy a mortal shell, I shall seek another...*"

In the hallway twisted animal shapes loped into sight, macabre amalgamations of metal and fur.

Marthir pulled Mortimer's face around. "The demon is bound through something else. Something beyond the form of the child. Think!"

The pain of his broken ribs and impaled hand clouded Mortimer's mind. *Something material, something solid... like stone.*

"Tara? Tara, are you..?"

A pool of blood spread from Tara's pinned body. The blades had gone through her and into the floor, the weight of the metal column pinning her like a fly. Little red bubbles came from her mouth. Beyond her the animals shuffled into the kitchen, metal teeth bared in snarls.

"The stone. From the altar. Where is it?"

With painful slowness Tara raised her hand and pointed at the hearth. Mortimer squinted, and saw in the centre of the chimney breast a square stone with engraved runes. As he lay pinned to Marthir he sighed in frustration.

Marthir followed his gaze and her features set hard.

"Have faith, Mortimer."

Her body transformed beneath him, rising into the air with a gush of blood. With one vault, Marthir's equine form had cleared the kitchen and the mutated animals. Mortimer dangled from her rump, pinned by the sword through his hand. His other free hand grasped down and tore the null-blade from the corpse of Aron.

"*No!*"

The demon's cry became a scream as Marthir dipped and scraped to a halt. Mortimer flipped over Marthir's back, his impaled hand shredding loose from the sword. In a spatter of blood he plunged the null-blade into the cursed stone. The scream permeated every inch of the house, shaking all occupants like an angry child would a rag doll.

The animals collapsed like discarded marionettes, metal running in rivulets from their lolling mouths. Then all was silent.

With a judder, Marthir returned to her human form. The sword had slid from her side, and she pressed on the wound. Mortimer gritted his teeth, and stemmed the pouring blood from his wounded hand, before collapsing against the druid.

"Child's play," Marthir said.

Mortimer smiled as he slipped into unconsciousness.

11.

Shrill sounds of birdsong dragged Mortimer from fevered dreams of furious priests and knotted whips. A beam of sunlight pinned him to a soft bed, and he squinted against the glare until a curvaceous figure stepped before it.

"It's always been my experience that Goldorian men favour sleep over all else."

Mortimer's chuckle was rewarded by knives of pain through his ribs. He groaned and pressed his chest with a bandaged hand.

"And that precludes more entertaining methods of convalescence."

With effort, Mortimer spoke. "Your husband…is Goldorian. As a matter of honour…I must offer…my life to him, and…"

"Oh, hush. My estranged husband hasn't seen me since I left to become a druid. Given that he is a blasphemous Wild Mage as well, your offer of recompense would end with you strapped to a stake and flames tickling your toes."

Mortimer rubbed his face in exasperation. Could this get any more damning? He'd made love to a changeling druid who was married to a Goldorian warlock. A terrible thought gripped him.

"Dear Mortis, you're not with child, are you?"

Marthir's laughter was as musical as the bird's chorus. She wiped a tear of mirth away. "Men! More worried about getting lasses in the family way than being torched for heresy. No, you're spared, Mortimer. It's the gift and curse of Nolir that her priestesses enjoy lovemaking yet remain barren. A beautiful irony."

There were tears in Marthir's eyes as she glanced away.

Much of Marthir's faith sits uneasy with her. We're alike in that respect.

"So...what now?" Mortimer asked.

"For my part? I'll not push my luck further remaining in Goldoria, lest the Inquisition sends others to seek you. I wouldn't want you to have to make a...public choice."

"So you return to Artoria?"

"To the Great Forest. The evil has been vanquished—by claw and sword, by bone and metal."

As Marthir rose, Mortimer asked, "The mines. How did you escape?"

"The beam shifting opened up a crevice on the other side of our little love den. I crawled through, though I thought my back was broken. It led to the passages, and I managed to find my way to the surface. Seems I was destined to keep saving you."

Mortimer smiled. With a laugh, Marthir turned and kissed him firmly. He ignored the searing pain in his ribs and hand.

"But that needs to stay a secret," Marthir said. "I have a reputation to maintain after all."

12.

"And that is my confession, Revered Father," Mortimer said. "In pursuing my mission, I have sinned again and again. Consorted with a changeling, allied with a druid. And in doing so, in compromising the teachings of Mortis above, we prevailed. The greater evil is gone."

The elderly priest leaned back against the wooden pew. Motes of dust danced in the light from the stained glass window of the chapel. Mortimer stared at the bandage around his hand in silence.

"And no one knows of your sins, of the blasphemy?"

"The mother, Tara, had passed by the time I awoke. The druid left her body and that of the child for me to perform a makeshift service. I pray her soul will find solace in her last-minute redemption."

"And is that what you seek, Sir Mortimer? Redemption?"

Anger flared in Mortimer's eyes. "I accept my sin. It was necessary. For my mission. Yet I could not allow a secret to fester in my heart."

"Even the most pious have secrets, Mortimer."

With a smooth motion, the priest drew his gnarled hand across his face. The beard and some strange waxy material peeled loose, revealing narrow vulpine features.

Mortimer's heart sank.

"Lurfir."

The Holy Assassin smiled coldly. "Sometimes we must weigh the sins against the greater good. The Sacred Knife know this, even if the Goldorian Knights do not."

"Then my secret…"

"Should remain so, until your deathbed, which I hope will be some time off. For there's much work to be done."

Lurfir rose with Mortimer, and the pair walked across the beams of light illuminating the nave of the chapel.

"Welcome to the Inquisition."

IF I HAVE TO SPELL IT OUT
By Marilyn Rucker

Hey Coz,

Thanks a lot for the email. Nice to hear from you again after all these months. But since you ask, no, it's not a good time for you to come visit. You may have forgotten what it's like out here at the cabin in the spring, since you haven't visited in years. But just to remind you, it's the rainy season. That means don't come. Because when I say rainy, I mean that in the next few weeks the rain will be dropping out of the sky in foot-thick sheets of water so solid they might as well be ice.

If you're walking to the cabin from the train station when that water hits you, it will smash you down into Owl Creek. You'll be stunned from the impact, so you won't be able to fight it off. You'll be dragged down beneath the rising creek water, and you'll bash your head into the rocks. The rocks will rip all your clothes off down to your damned underwear, and they'll tear most of your skin off while they're at it. This will all happen faster than a gnat blinks. You won't be able to stop it.

Then you'll be dead, and it will have happened so fast you won't even know why. And your ghost will wander the woods around my cabin, complaining and mewling about how you don't know what the hell happened. And you'll be mad at me for not meeting you at the train station.

Then, since I won't want you haunting me for the rest of my life, I'll have to come out with my smudge sticks and dance around my cabin skyclad. Damned if I'm going to dance naked in front of my spoiled, baby cousin, even if it is to direct his soul home. I'm sorry, but that's just how I feel. Especially when you (or, I guess, your ghost) will probably be wearing that damned Confederate flag underwear you always wore in middle school like some damned stupid white supremacist. You're probably wearing them right now, the exact same pair you wore in eighth grade. Yes, that is a crack about your lack of physical growth, which is eclipsed only by your lack of personal hygiene. But I digress. Sorry Coz.

Anyway, your soul will be wandering around lost because you, as usual, wouldn't listen to me about the rainy season, and I will have to come out and exorcise you. And yes, it will be a big pain in my butt, but what's new about that? I've always had to pull your sorry ass out of trouble.

Remember when we were kids and I'd be stuck carrying you around and making sure you didn't eat Grandma's hemlock stash? This was, of course, while all my friends in town were out having fun and going to movies and having social lives. And I never got paid a dime to make up for my wasted summers watching you. Why should anything change now?

I'm sorry to be so blunt with you, Chris. As you know, I've always been honest. I'm sure you'll think I'm just being spiteful, but oh well. No means no. So don't come see me or bad things will happen!

Much Love From Your Older and Wiser Cousin,
Charlotte

Hey Much Older But Not Proportionately Wiser Cousin Harlotte,

Yeah, I get that you're still spiteful, um…honest. You're also still incredibly rude and inhospitable. I don't know why you think it's okay to be so bitchy. I'm nice to you when you visit, even though you don't deserve it. Remember I let you stay with me last Samhain? I took you to see my new office and bought you a nice lunch. Because that's what family does when family comes to visit. I know you were just there to see Aunt Margaret, but still. I took the time to hang out with you. And Deedie's is an expensive restaurant. You should know—you ordered the sea bass.

And you repaid me by helping me lose my job, remember? And yes, I know you're going to say you were just trying to help, but you completely misread the situation. You could have just asked me before you started meddling, but you just always think you know best, don't you?

Why the hell did you think I wanted to sleep with Jessica? She's my boss. I didn't want that love charm put in her coffee. She was all over me for months! She wouldn't let me get any work done. It was embarrassing. And her husband threatened to tear my privates off and stuff me like a turducken. I didn't merely have to quit—I had to leave town and change my cellphone number. I had to erase my existence in Cedar Falls. I had to kill a virgin goat to lock in the anonymity charm.

Do you know how hard it is to find a certified virgin goat?

Why couldn't you let me handle my love life myself? I know how to make a simple attraction charm. I like to be subtle and leave most of the work up to nature. But subtle is completely lost on you. And that's if I'd even wanted to sleep with the woman, which I didn't! Yes, I liked her. Yes, you absolutely picked up on that and misread it as a sexual thing. And then you had to butt in and try to make it all work for me, because you're a complete control freak.

Just being honest, not spiteful, Coz.

Jessica was the first really good boss I ever had. She liked my work and was helping me advance my career in marketing. I was making good money and enjoying my work for a change. I had a chance to do something with my life besides become an impoverished hedge witch like you or Grandma. And no offense, but really I would rather live a middle class lifestyle. I like cheeseburgers and first run movies a whole lot better than fried tree snakes and wild onions and campfire tales.

If I didn't know better, Char, I would think you were jealous of my life. I think you hexed me so that I'd have to come live with you. Because you couldn't stand to see me doing so well. Or maybe you're lonely. I'd give it even odds, but you're acting so psychotic about my coming, I guess maybe you didn't ruin my life on purpose. You're not showing any guilt about it at all. But you've always stunk at the whole remorse thing.

But whether you care or not, you've managed to deprive me of a job and a place I can afford to live. I have no choice now but to come stay with you in what is not just yours but *our* family home. As Grandma told all of us, we are all welcome there for the rest of our lives. Just because you've chosen to squat there and hardly ever leave doesn't mean you're the only one who gets to live in it.

By the way, if you throw a drowning curse at me, you're going to suffer some seriously painful consequences. That's how you're supposed to make a threat, Coz. You keep it vague and unspecified so you can leave your options open. You don't bind yourself up with prophecy or destiny. You don't use the stupid, deadly rain and water and rocks tirade you used on Matt Hannaby when he was throwing dog turds at us down by the bridge. He was stupid enough to believe you. But I'm not buying it. You never were any good at water magic.

I already know you're going to say the love charm on Jessica was just a joke. But it really wasn't funny. Thanks to you, I'm jobless and homeless. So you're just going to have to put up with my opinions and my little foibles, and I don't really want to hear any more crap about how you put up with me as a kid. There is no way in Odin's realm that it is anywhere near as bad as having to put up with you in any stage of your development.

Sorry if that's harsh, but I'm just being honest.

Also, I know all about water magic. I can summon it, repel it, and even (gasp) use an umbrella so I can walk through it without getting wet or even uttering one spell.

I'll be at the train station at 3:05 on Saturday. Come get me at the station. I know you still have Grandma's old Civic. If you conveniently forget so that I'm forced to walk to the cabin, reconsider that threat of sending a murderous creek after me. Please keep in mind that I still remember how to cast a truly nasty herpes spell. Remember your drama camp dance? Or what should have been your drama camp dance?

Burningly, Itchingly, and Stingingly,
Christopher

Hey Crystal Balls,

So there you'll be, all dead and drowned and confused, and I'll have to chant the exorcism rite and sing the songs and then the Heavens will open and your spirit guide, who will probably be Great-Great-Grandpa John-Bob, will come down. And contrary to what you might think, he won't approve of that nasty Confederate underwear you're still wearing on the skinny white ass of your skinny white ghost body. Because although he fought for the Confederacy, it was only because he was drafted and they'd have hung him if he hadn't.

And he'll say in a voice that will chill the marrow in your bones and raise the hairs on your underdeveloped gonads like the quills of a fretful porpetine:

"Christopher, why the hell don't you ever listen to anyone? Why didn't you just stay away when your cousin asked you nicely? Don't you know you're a fucking idiot?"

And you'll just look at him and whine and say "Why you calling me mean names?"

And he'll say "Because you're so stupid nothing else registers. That's why you're dead!"

Then he'll slap you on the head with his hat, as he was known to do in life, according to family legend. And then he'll take you to your reward, if you can call it that. I would not get all excited about that. You have not been particularly good or bad in this life, which does not bode well for you. You're going to the boring place. So sorry.

Regretfully (Yawn),
Charlotte

Hey Chunklette,

First of all, I am not going to the boring place, although I admit that staying with you will be abysmally dull. But in suffering through some time with you, I'll experience the afterlife as a place of verdant and splendid beauty simply by comparison.

And, for your information, I no longer wear Confederate flag underpants. I had the one pair in eighth grade, and that was only because I liked Daisy Duke. I do not wear them anymore. I do not long for the rise of the old South and slavery. I am not a white supremacist asshole. But thanks for the subtle implication.

And you don't have to tell me about our great-great-grandpa, John Robert Templeton. You know Dad always told me I was just like him. Meaning I'm scarier, meaner, and more determined to "do my duty" than anyone else in the world. I am also stubborn and deeply impatient with stupidity. You are not going to scare me out of coming home. And yes, you are going to let me work with you at the farmer's market. I anticipate expansion into a web-based business, supported by some extensive telemarketing. We can sell Grandma's remedies and herbs worldwide. I have some good ideas, or at least Jessica thought so. Too bad you pissed all over that option for me.

Did my dad ever tell you the story about Great-Great-grandpa John-Bob's leg?

He told me that Grandpa John-Bob, reluctant Confederate though he was, still killed about twenty Yankees, dutifully defending some cornfield in Tennessee. Then he got his leg blown off. But he didn't just lie there on the ground bleeding out. No, he crawled over fifty yards to get that leg, past a lot of other scattered body parts and screaming men. And when he got to his leg, he grabbed it and held it on his chest till the medics came and got him, and he insisted that they let him keep it. Usually they threw all the arms and legs on a fire and burned 'em up, but he wouldn't hear of it. Told the doctors he'd roast them in hell if they threw a perfectly good leg away. They believed him. He was a scary son of a bitch, even near death as he was.

He was discharged, and so then he had to limp back home, and he carried the leg with him in a bag on his back the whole way. It smelled pretty bad by the time he got home. Then he went and buried it in the family graveyard out back of the house. He even gave it its own little silk hose as a kind of shroud. And he dug a grave and had a ceremony. Said he'd be joining it in good time but that he had a little more living he needed to do. You know the grave, Chunks. It's the one with the tiny little headstone that says "Jr." on it. Our great-grampa had a wry sense of humor.

Then, of course, he got busy with Great-Great-Grandma, and they had a few kids, which is why you and I are even here. And when he died, Great-Great-Grammy buried him in a grave right next to the one his leg was in. She didn't put him in the same hole as his leg because she was afraid of that leg. She didn't want to dig it up to put it in with him.

She had a terror of that disembodied leg that lasted long after Great-Great-Grandpa died. She was afraid that leg would scratch its way up through the ground with its moldy, gangrenous toes and come crawling along like some kind of crazy snake and wreak revenge on her for not joining it back up with Grandpa John-Bob in the same grave. Maybe cover her head with the hose it was buried in and strangle her on it. She had a special terror of that, for some reason.

Funny, she wasn't afraid of Grandpa John-Bob's body coming after her when she buried him. I never could figure that out. I mean, that main grave was where his head and his heart and his other organs were buried, which is what you'd think would actually want to mete out revenge. And really, if the leg could dig its way up out of the grave, why couldn't it just dig over to Grandpa's body and settle on down next to it, kind of like a pup. That's what Great-Great-grandma said she hoped would happen, if the leg took a mind to wander. But Dad told me it always bothered her that the graves were just a few hundred feet from where we all slept.

Dad didn't tell you that story, did he? 'Cause you were always so goosey about ghosts. I bet he didn't want to scare his little niece. So how is it living right next to the family graveyard, Char?

Isn't the leg still there in its lonely little grave? Have you heard anything moving under the earth over there just a few hundred feet from where you sleep? Do you think the leg found its way to Grandpa John-Bob's dead body, or is it wandering around under the dirt looking for it? Think it's crawling through the dirt nearer and nearer the house? Think it's going to find its way to your bedroom and rustle its way up to you?

Maybe you ought to reconsider trying to scare me off and beg me to come help you scare off Grampa's leg. I can do that, you know. I'm good at charming the dead. And I ain't afraid of no hose.

Don't Look but Junior is Crawling Up Your Leg,
Christopher

Hey Pissy Chrissy (remember when you got so scared you wet yourself at your first midnight ritual and you had to change your robes before we could go on?),

I am not "goosey about ghosts." I have surpassed even Grandma in power, and I am quite capable of subduing a simple human haunt, or even a partial haunt. I do not, however, claim to have control over all nature. I'm trying to warn you that things are far more difficult at the house since you last visited. And I have been having too many visitors, as I said. Great-Uncle Ethan was here for weeks, and I just got him to leave. You can imagine the amount of negativity he just dumped all over the house. It's not pretty.

And, Chris, you attract negativity. You can't help it, but I don't need more of it right now. And no, I don't think you can help with cleaning things up. You were never good at that. Mainly because you always say you'll help clean up, and you don't. Think back. Do you even know how to wash a dish by hand? I've never seen it. And have you ever once been the one preparing and then burning the smudge sticks for astral cleansing? I've not seen that either.

Anyway, I am not just trying to scare you off. These problems with the rainy season are not my doing. It's a whole lot rougher in the woods than it used to be. The magic is stronger and more dangerous. Maybe it's global warming. Maybe it's the Republicans. I don't know. But I am trying to apprise you of the hazards that have grown more intense around the house since the last time you visited. For example, in addition to our extremely dangerous thunderstorms and flash floods, we are also having trouble with mosquitoes. They are otherworldly in both their size and vehemence. They are bigger around than Great-Uncle Dan's fist when he was whipping us with his "Billy Bob's" belt buckle, and they're almost as mean as him too.

If you don't have the right charms established and supplement with a substantial amount of Deep Woods Repel Spray, Pissy Chrissy, they'll gang up on you and swarm you away to their scum-covered larvae pond. They won't kill you right away either. They're sentient and murderous. They'll let you drink the scummy water, enough to stay alive, and then they'll drink a little of you at a time to make you last. They're like vampires in that respect, I guess. Except they don't turn their victims into one of them. Well, not unless you count them laying eggs all over you so the new hatched larvae have a blood meal to eat. Their particular species is partial to that.

So even if you don't drown in the rains, you're going to get literally eaten alive walking through the woods to get here. I've got a spell I can sing that works for me, but it relies heavily on intonation. You couldn't sing it at all 'cause you can't carry a tune if it was tied to your butt.

And no, I don't have the Civic anymore, so I can't just come pick you up. I had to sell the car because, as you've inferred, business is not booming. But that is not due to any mismanagement on my part. And you can't just horn in on my farmer's market booth because that's my only source of income and there is only so much sassafras and wheat grass juice that the market will demand, and it has demanded very little lately.

I am sorry about that Jessica business. I truly am, but it wasn't my fault it didn't work out. You just weren't able to take advantage of a great opportunity. That woman would have covered you in cheeseburgers and taken you to movies for the rest of your life. You should have let her have you and spoil you like the little rotten kid you are, you blind moron!

But I understand. You blew your one chance at happiness, and you are broke and homeless. I know that I'm your family. I know I'm obligated to take you in. But it's still not a good time to come. You're still going to have to be very careful.

Maybe you can survive the rains and the mosquitoes and the ghosts of our ancestors. I don't know about the rest of it. The Windigoes like to come out at night still, but they rarely eat people these days. Most of my neighbors just leave a McRib meal out, when McRibs are in season, and that tends to satisfy their bloodlust. They also like Wonderburgers with mustard. Better buy a few Wondermeals before you get on the train in Cedar Falls, because the Wonderburger in town got overwhelmed by Windigoes raiding their supply trucks.

Just make sure to have 'em cook the meat rare and bloody and leave the bags open and on their side so the Windigoes know it's for them. Otherwise they're going to tear out your eyes and drink your brain through the sockets like they always do.

But otherwise, if you decide to ignore all my warnings and you survive these obstacles and you make it to the front porch, I'm looking forward to seeing you. It's always fun, even if you are a brat.

If you go through Fredericksburg on your way to the station, pick me up some of that peach brandy at Flickerson's down on 290. We can put it on some ice cream. And then if you insist, we can go dig up poor old Grandpa John-Bob's leg and reunite it with Grandpa. Maybe he and his leg won't jump out at us and make you pee all over yourself. Maybe if you bring your umbrella he'll be so impressed he'll just stay resting in peace.

Hugs and Kisses
Charlotte

Hey Char,

I've already picked up some peach brandy for you. Do not curse the train or the weather and do not sic the Windigoes on me. I'll be there on Saturday, just like I said.

Love you too,
Christopher

A HAUNTED CASTLE
By Lisa Zhang Wharton

"I hear this castle is haunted," whispered Sam. He was a tall and lean, a teenager of fifteen. His family was visiting southern Germany from St. Paul, Minnesota for their vacation.

He and a group of five other teenagers sat on lawn chairs on the neatly cut green lawn next to a medieval castle, Brennhausen. The castle was a tall and majestic, made of stone with red tile roof surrounded by a moat, farmland and a large forest. It had been around for more than 800 years.

The sky was blue, with a few clouds resembling a herd of sheep. A large shadow was cast by the immense castle, but the teenagers stayed on the east side where the sun shone.

"No. I grew up visiting here every summer. I've never seen any ghosts or demons," said Lorenz. He was sixteen and would be one of future owners of the castle. He was lying on a stretch-out lawn chair, half asleep. "But that would be great, if it were true." He sat up. "Life can be boring here."

"How could life be boring in a castle?" asked Sam. He and Lorenz were second cousins, but it was the first time he'd come to visit.

"You'll see. After a week, the castle will be too old, the moat too murky, and the rowboat too small. Plus, we have all these annoying nettles, right? Chloe?" Lorenz turned to Sam's half-sister, who had been here once before, as Lorenz's sister Anna's companion.

As usual she had buried her nose in a thick book. Chloe was thirteen, and a pretty girl with long brown hair. A pair of black glasses made her look smart, which the others thought was redundant. "What?" She raised her head from the book and stared at her cousin.

"Never mind. As long as there are books around, you will never be bored, correct?" Lorenz asked.

Chloe nodded.

Max, a boy of twelve, ran to Lorenz' side. "Do you hear the dogs barking? Our caretakers just bought some Rottweilers. They're planning to train them as attack dogs." The boy was slightly overweight, with his round face and curly hair making him an instant clown. He was followed by Stefan. Both boys were Lorenz's bothers, with whom Lorenz would have to share ownership of the castle.

He would be required to share, even though Lorenz was named after his most famous ancestor, Lorenz, the Duke and Prince-Bishop of Wurzburg, an important city in Bavaria. Unfortunately, their sister Anna would get nothing because girls were not allowed to own property back in medieval times and sadly for her, time stood still in the countryside of Bavaria.

"Max, you're up early," said Lorenz.

"Yes. The Rottweilers woke me up." Max shook back his long, messy hair. He had dressed in an ancient Egyptian Pharaoh's outfit, his favorite costume.

"That's the most exciting thing I've heard today." Lorenz stood up. "Maybe we should visit these vicious Rottweilers."

"Let's go. What are we waiting for?" Stefan, the oldest brother, was an impatient seventeen-year-old.

"Shouldn't we ask our parents?" said Chloe. She was often the most responsible of the group.

"Don't wreck our fun." Sam stood up. "Let's go."

The other girl, Anna, spoke. "No. Mom said we should go and do the rowboat first and show our cousins Nettle Island." She was an attractive girl of fourteen. Sam had discovered that she was a little bossy.

"Okay," said Lorenz. He always tried to imagine what his ancestor would do in a given situation. In this case, it would be "obey his mom's order."

They ran to the moat and undid the rope that tied the rowboat to the dock.

"Ladies, first," said Stefan. Anna and Chloe carefully jumped into the boat and Stefan pushed them away. As soon as they were pushed out into the moat, Chloe pulled her book from her bag and began reading while Anna was rowed.

"Let's use the canoe," said Lorenz.

"But we have four people and only one canoe," said Max.

"No problem. I can swim over to the Nettle Island," said Sam, who was a great swimmer.

"Are you kidding? This is a moat—unlike the lakes in Minnesota, it is actually quite muddy and full of fertilizers from the surrounding farms," said Stefan.

"Stefan and Max, you two can take Sam in the canoe. I can stay ashore and watch," said Lorenz.

"Sam, you sit in the front and I'll stay in the back steering. Max, you can sit in the middle, so the weight is balanced. We don't want the boat bow or stern heavy," said Stefan.

"Stop making fun of Max. He is most helpful sometimes," said Lorenz, but even he smiled a little. They often laughed when they thought of Max and his clownish demeanor.

Stefan brought over a nice wooden canoe, decorated with a lively red dragon and two oars engraved with ducks.

"What a beautiful boat." Sam while stepped in carefully and slowly walked to the front, where he down.

"It was a gift from a Bavarian king, so it's quite an honor to ride in it," said Lorenz.

Stefan jumped in and sat in the back seat holding one oar while Sam was holding the other.

"It's your turn, Max," Stefan ordered.

Max walked toward the edge of the dock and tried very carefully to step in. Unfortunately, as one leg reached the inside of the canoe, he stumbled. The canoe flipped, and the three boys fell into the moat.

Lorenz helped them out of the water, all the boys laughing and groaning. They could hear Anna and Chloe's loud hoots in the distance.

"My costume!" Max was devastated.

"Max, go back and change. Then we can have a peaceful boat outing," said Lorenz.

"Sure." Max left, looking sheepish.

Eventually, they arrived at the Nettle Island. To their disappointment, the nettles were right at the water's edge, which meant they couldn't push each other toward shore without getting wet again.

Once on the shore of the small wooded island, the group played "Hide and Seek." The small size of the island made the game quite a challenge. Being the most resourceful, Sam actually dug a hole near the water's edge to hide in, getting stung by the nettles in the process. Even so, it was great fun.

After the little adventure to Nettle Island, Sam, Lorenz and Chloe once again sat on the lawn chairs, resting in the courtyard next to castle's main entrance. Both of Sam's ankles were covered with bandages so he couldn't scratch the rash caused by the nettles. Chloe still read her book and Lorenz stared at the sky, which had rather interesting clouds, which he said reminded him of a herd of galloping horses.

"Lorenz, are you counting the sheep?" asked Sam, who held a book on his lap.

"Yes—but they're horses. Trying to ward off my boredom."

"Or it is a symptom of boredom? We did have an exciting morning," said Sam.

"Ok. It was above average," said Lorenz.

"You are kidding, aren't you?" said Sam, with some disbelief. "Yeah, it must be boring not to be stung by nettles. Max's falling into the moat should have made your day. It certainly made mine."

"We're fortunate to have him as a brother," agreed Lorenz. "Anna could pull off some crazy schemes, too. Once she hid in the dungeon for a whole day and no one could find her. Mom almost called the police, so it's not always boring. One year toward the end of the summer, a farmer showed up with hundreds of sheep. They were on their way home to spend the winter. We chased the sheep all over the place. It was the highlight of the summer."

Sam stood up and snatched Chloe's book away, earning him a dirty look. "I have an idea. We should have a costume party. Then we'll turn off the lights, and tell everyone it's actually a Hide and Seek game. We will hide and the adults will have to look for us," said Sam. He had played many Hide and Seek games in their house back in Minnesota.

"Sure. I can wear my Marie Antoinette costume." All of sudden, Chloe was excited.

"I will be Count Dracula," said Sam. "I saw a costume room on the very top floor where you have to go via bare stone staircases."

"You've been there already?" Lorenz seemed surprised, and a little disappointed.

"Cousin Max showed me. We were looking for swords to practice fencing but found some ancient bows and arrows instead," said Sam.

"I bet he's practicing archery right now," said Lorenz. "Ok. You go and round up Max. I'll go and find Anna and Stefan."

"Okay."

Both Sam and Lorenz stood up and left Chloe there all by herself.

It turned out Stefan, Max and Anna were at the family playground nearby. Anna was swinging and singing "Somewhere Over the Rainbow." She was even dressed like Dorothy in the "Wizard of Oz".

Max was aiming at a target about twenty feet away with the ancient bow and arrow.

"Hurry up," said Stefan, who was always impatient. "Why does it take you so long to aim?" He threw a rock at the target.

"You're messing me up," said Max, irritation showing on his red face.

"I'm giving you an extra challenge," replied Stefan.

"Okay, you can have it." Max threw the bow and arrow on the ground, intending to walk away.

Sam blocked his path. "Hey, don't go. I have a plan. How about we organize a costume party and then turn the lights off so we can play Hide and Seek?"

"A costume party? I want to be Darth Vader." Stefan dropped the bow and arrow and walked over.

"I thought there were only ancient costumes. I heard they had many costume parties 400 hundred years ago in the castle." Sam felt proud to know a few things about the ancient property.

"I know. This is my grandfather's castle. The castle is at least 800 years old. It was awarded to our family in 1681 through a law suit. Our family was already very powerful back then," said Stefan. "I put the Darth Vader costume there myself last year. You think you invented the costume party?" He paused and then said, "But a costume party combined with a Hide and Seek game is an ingenious invention." He patted Sam's shoulder.

"Stop showing off, Stefan," Lorenz shouted.

"Sure. You always act like our great ancestor, the Duke and Prince-Bishop Lorenz since you're named after him. You're a walking trophy yourself." The others thought Stefan sounded a little jealous.

To defuse the tension, Sam turned to Max who, among many other talents, was also an Egyptologist. "Who do you want to be?"

"I want to be the King Pharaoh if my costume dries up in time," said Max.

"I want to be Cleopatra," said Anna.

"Not Dorothy?" asked Stefan

"No. Dorothy is too cute. I want to be a powerful woman." She let out a powerful shriek, to prove it.

"Let's announce it at the dinner time!" Lorenz sounded like a true leader. Maybe he was the reincarnation of his ancestor, the Duke and Prince-Bishop Lorenz.

Sam's parents, Ryan and Helen, were in the kitchen helping their hosts, Kim and Hans, prepare dinner. Two pans of Lasagna were baking in the oven. Helen made a salad while Ryan whipped up a chocolate cake. Kim made macaroni and cheese for the kids.

"How was your outing today?" asked Kim. She was a medium sized woman with long, silky blond hair.

Sam's mother, Helen, said, "It was wonderful. I'm glad the kids didn't come along. We were able to visit many churches and Monasteries in one day. Thank you so much for babysitting the kids."

"No sweat. They took care of themselves. Except for three of them falling into the moat, there was no other excitement." Kim was used to raising four kids of her own.

"I love the Baroque styled churches the most. They're the most colorful and expressive." Helen, who had come from Beijing, China about 20 years before, still was taking in the luxurious life style of the western world. And on top of it, the opulent life of western aristocrats had definitely astonished her. But, like her son, she was ready to embrace it and could get used to it easily. Growing up in the era of Mao's Cultural Revolution, she felt she deserved something better. "What I like the most was the imitation marble inside the churches. It looks so real."

"Do you remember why they're not made of real marble?" asked Ryan. Sam's father was the tallest man in the room and had a degree in architecture.

"It was the style of the time. Hans told me," said Helen. "Thank you, Hans. You are the most patient tour guide."

"I thought the Baroque style was definitely a treat for everyone's eyes," said Ryan. "But for me, they were too gaudy."

"Don't be so critical." Helen nudged Ryan playfully.

"I said it was a visual treat for everyone's eyes. For my mind, I preferred the Gothic style Monastery that held the remains of Hans' family ancestors," said Ryan, grinning.

"Gothic style is too gloomy for me," said Helen. She turned to Kim. "I think it is interesting that the family of Queen Elizabeth of England came from this region."

"It was a political marriage," said Ryan.

"All royal marriages were political back then. But not anymore. The marriage between Hans and I was definitely not political, right Hans?" Kim turned to her husband who sliced the homemade bread.

"I thought it was!" Hans said in a deadpan voice.

Everyone laughed.

The entire family and guests sat in thick leather chairs with heavy wooden frames, gathered around an immense wooden table. Sam loved the chairs because they felt smooth from several hundred years of rubbing by people who sat on them.

Lorenz stood up and made his announcement. "Let's meet in the ballroom after dinner in costumes. We're having a costume party."

"Will Chloe play the piano?" asked Grandma Peggy, an energetic 75 years old with short grey hair and wearing an elegant dress of red lace.

"Of course. Anna will sing, too," said Lorenz.

"Who said I'll sing? I'll shriek, instead. Get ready to put on your earplugs," said Anna.

"I'll turn off my hearing aids," said Grandpa Wilhelm, who was the owner of the castle and a real Duke. Yet he was the most modest person in the room.

"Who wants to join in?" asked Lorenz.

Everyone raised their hands except for Wilhelm. "Someone has to remain clear-headed amidst all the fun," he said quietly.

"I'll stay here with you," said Peggy. Their family thought them the most loving couple in the world.

Lorenz and kids disappeared immediately after the meal.

The teenagers gathered up in the fourth floor ballroom, wearing costumes, and standing in a circle next to the grand piano. A few chairs had been pushed to the side and the curtains were not drawn. They hoped the natural light would flood in when the lights were turned off.

"What are we waiting for?" asked Stefan. "We have to plan our action."

"Yes. We should turn off the lights before adults arrive," whispered Sam.

"Then what do we do?" asked Max.

"Chloe starts playing spooky music and Anna shrieks scary songs. The rest of us will hide," said Lorenz. "Do we all agree?"

"Yes!" Everyone raised their hands.

"Stefan, you go with Sam to turn the circuit breaker off," said Lorenz.

"Sure. "Stefan and Sam spoke in unison, and raced down the rug-covered stairs.

"I assume you know where it is," asked Sam, going as quickly as he could.

"Of course, I grew up here. It's in the dungeon," Stefan whispered.

"Dungeon?" asked Sam. "How interesting."

"You haven't been there yet?" Stefan looked a little surprised.

"No. Now is my chance." Sam's voice gave away his excitement.

"It's dark and damp down there. Good. You have a flashlight. There are many empty cider bottles. My ancestors hid homemade apple cider and even Jews down there during the two world wars. I'm sure some people died there, which is why we sometimes hear howling in the evening," said Stefan. He turned toward Sam, gauging his reaction.

"I'm not afraid," said Sam.

Stefan pushed the wooden door open. It swung open with a loud creak, and they walked out into the courtyard. The night was moonless, pitch dark, and quiet as well. The lovely horse clouds from earlier in the day had turned thick and dark. The Rottweilers must be sleeping, said Sam to himself. He followed Stefan to a wrought iron door on the other side of the castle.

They had to push really hard to open it. Once inside, they walked down a few steps made of wooden blocks. With Sam's flashlight, they were able see where they were going.

"Are you scared?" asked Stefan, hoping his cousin was.

"No. As long as there are no Rottweiler attack dogs."

"You're afraid. I can see your flashlight shaking," teased Stefan.

They came to a wrought iron switch with a wooden handle, about two feet long on a box mounted on the wall.

"Okay. Are you ready?" Stefan tried to pull the handle down. It was stiff, and wouldn't move. Sam joined with his free hand. With both lending their strength, the breaker gave way, and the lights in the castle switched off. Even though they couldn't see it, they could feel it.

They did a high five in the dark.

"I can hear them screaming," said Sam, grinning.

"No, you don't. You're imagining it. Let's get out of here." Stefan ran upstairs and outside. Sam followed. It was even darker and quieter than before, as though everything had gone dead along with the light. Fortunately they had the flashlight.

They found the door and snuck in. The castle was deadly quiet inside too, which surprised them. Where was the chaos caused by their recently manmade catastrophe? At first, Sam felt alarmed, but then he heard whispers and footsteps. As he and Stefan walked up the stairs, they heard music and singing.

"Everything seems to be going as planned," whispered Sam.

"Sound like they're having fun. I can't wait to join them," said Stefan, and went faster.

"You're right. They're not bored anymore." Sam quickened his steps, too.

When they arrived at the ballroom door, what they saw went beyond their wildest imaginings.

Chloe's blue Marie Antoinette dress had turned into a ragged drape of black and grey. Her hair had become long, and stringy, and her eyes glowed like two light bulbs. She played a song from the Adam's Family, laughing hysterically, surprising Sam. Was this his little sister Chloe?

Anna, Stefan's little sister, was no longer Cleopatra. She had become a witch with long curly hair, huge bulging eyes and big yellow protruding teeth.

Sam inched forward as though pushing through a crowd. The room was filled darkness, and he was filled with uncertainty. He entered the ballroom, and nearly cried out.

It was too unreal for him to comprehend. He blinked, but still saw six nuns suspended in midair, singing happily. He looked closely, seeing his parents, Stefan's parents, and the grandparents.

"Oh, my god. This castle is haunted." Sam called out, "Can anyone hear me?"

No one heard him and no one cared, going about their own business.

Or their own wildness.

"Shhh!" Stefan put one of his hands over Sam's mouth. He pointed to Sam's chest.

Sam touched his chest, then his neck and finally his teeth.

"Oh…I grew fangs." He realized his hands had grown cold, and hard as marble. "I've turned into a real vampire. I'm really Dracula!" For some reason, the events of the evening no longer seemed strange. He turned toward Stefan and asked, "How about you?"

"I'm still just Count Olaf," said Stefan.

"Would you like to be a Count Dracula?" Sam moved closer to Stefan, approaching his neck with his fangs.

Stefan stepped away, fearing what was about to happen, and disappearing into the darkness.

Hearing a scream from the floor above, Sam decided to check upstairs. He found Max in a small bedroom. The boy stood with both hands covered with honey.

"Look what I found!" Max licked the honey.

"Where did that come from?" asked Sam, a little puzzled. Honey bees in middle of the castle? How peculiar....

"It seeps through the wall." Max pointed toward the wall behind him.

 Sam looked closely and saw what Max meant. Sticky honey dripped down the wall. It was one of the more rustic bedrooms with no wallpaper, allowing the honey to seep freely. Then Sam saw that bees as well as honey invaded the tiny bedroom.

"Max, let's go." Sam tried to pull Max away. "See the bees? Can you hear the buzzing sound? You'll be stung."

"I saw them, which was why I screamed. But then I realize that wherever there is honey, there are bees. I was stung but it didn't bother me. I think I'm immune to bee stings." Max mumbled, his mouth glued together by honey. His honey-covered nose grew bigger, and his eyes became rounder and much larger. Thick hair appeared on his face.

The boy had turned into a bear, obsessed with eating honey.

Confused, Sam gave up and turned to leave. As he did, he noticed something even more disturbing, if that was possible.

The neighbor's attack dogs, the Rottweilers, had climbed the castle wall, looking through the windows at them. Each dog had bloodshot eyes, skinny droopy ears, and an incredibly long tongue. They stared at the two boys with great interest. Sam feared they could come in through the windows if they pushed hard enough.

He gathered up his courage and went closer to the window. He opened his mouth, showing his fangs. Seeing his hands had grown sharp nails, he waved them, threatening the dogs. He even let blood drip down the side of his mouth.

The dogs were not deterred. Instead, they became more excited. Max had hidden in the corner of the room, still sucking his fingers. At that moment, Sam felt the strongest urge to drink Max's blood. Honey didn't interest him at all. He needed blood.

He wanted to fight the Rottweilers.

But as a new vampire, he was unsure of his strength. It occurred to him that he had to warn others about the dogs. Together, they could work out a plan to get rid of them.

Sam dragged Max down to the ballroom, a floor below. He wished his sister and cousins weren't there, so he could suck Max dry first, before looking for them.

On the heels of that thought, he realized that how bad and dangerous that idea was.

Max was his cousin and he should protect him.

When they arrived in the ballroom, the music and singing stopped. The room was quiet except for the scratching sound on the windows made by the Rottweilers. Lorenz, Stefan, Anna and Chloe stood in a circle, staring at either other.

Then they noticed Sam which stirred them. "Where did you go? We looked everywhere for you," said Lorenz.

"Stay away from him! He's a vampire." Stefan took a step back. "He'll drink your blood."

"Come on—be serious," replied Sam, controlling himself. "Let's take care of the Rottweilers first."

"So, you wouldn't attack me then?" asked Stefan, in a shaky voice.

"Not right now." Sam saw the look on Stefan's face. "Oh, gosh. I'm just kidding," Maybe he was kidding.

"You should go out and fight the Rottweilers. You can suck their blood," said Stefan. "It would be bloody buffet for you

"I'm thinking about it. But we should work as a team," said Sam. Then he turned to Lorenz. "What do you think, Prince-Bishop?"

"You're right," said Lorenz calmly. "We should figure out a plan to deal with them."

"I can't think of anything better than sending Sam out there. Maybe I should go with him. I'm a bear now," said Max in a deep bearish voice. He licked the honey that remained around his mouth.

"I agree. Sam's desire for blood will give him enormous strength." said Stefan, rather seriously. "I trust him to do a good job and save everyone in Brennhausen."

"Oh stop, brother," said Lorenz. "Do you want to help?"

"How?" asked Stefan.

Lorenz asked, "What do dogs like?"

"They like meat," said Anna.

"Meat. You're right. We'll go up to the roof and throw the meat to the sky. The Rottweilers will leap for the meat and fall to their death," said Sam. Then I can go down and suck their blood dry, he thought.

"I can shoot them with the bow and arrow," offered Max.

"I could play scary music to frighten them," offered Chloe, who was no longer scared.

"We should never underestimate the power of the music." Lorenz encouraged her.

"Okay. Max. You find the bow and arrow. Sam and Stefan, you go to the kitchen and get all the meat we have. I will go up to the roof and check it out. We'll meet back here again in 15 minutes and go up to the roof together, as a squad," said Lorenz.

Sam thought Lorenz was a great leader just like his ancestor, the Prince-Bishop.

"How about Chloe and I?" asked Anna.

"Would you stay here and make scary music?" asked Lorenz.

"Okay." Anna turned to her cousin. "We can make it as scary as possible, right Chloe?"

Chloe jumped, looking startled. "Yes."

"Then we can come up to the roof and help, too, right?" asked Anna.

"Right," said Lorenz.

At that moment, no matter how vehemently the Rottweilers scratched at the windows, the teenagers were no longer frightened. They were a team now, holding each other's hands. Their eyes glowed, especially Chloe's. Nothing could scare them, and nothing would.

Not even the vicious Rottweilers.

After about fifteen minutes, Max returned with the bow and arrow. Sam and Stefan entered, carrying two bags of meat. The girls were still making music, which was quite scary.

Lorenz came down from the roof top, breathless and excited. "I found the perfect weapon for us." His grin split his face.

"What?" Anna stopped singing and grabbed her brother's shoulder, shaking him. "Come on. Don't make me guess."

"Yes, you have to guess. So what weapon did I find on the roof top?" Lorenz looked at Anna, still grinning.

"Swords," said Anna. She remembered Sam and Max had been searching for them earlier.

"Wrong," said Lorenz.

"That's easy," said Stefan. "A Cannon."

"Yes. You won the prize," said Lorenz.

"I don't want a prize. What's our plan?" Stefan couldn't wait to fight the Rottweilers.

"It's rather easy. We will bring the meat up to the roof top and use the cannon to shoot them into the sky. The Rottweilers will leap toward it and fall to their death," said Lorenz.

"I'll put one piece of meat on the arrow and shoot it toward the Rottweilers. They can eat the meat and the arrow at the same time," said Max.

That's exactly what had happened. Rottweilers began leaping to the meat in the air, one after another, falling to their death right after.

Lorenz wanted to try the cannon. They put the last chuck of the meat and three chickens into a bag, stuffed it into the cannon.

"I want to shoot," said Anna.

"You aren't afraid?" Lorenz asked.

"No. You should be afraid of me. I'm a real witch." She glowered at everyone with her big bulging eyes and sharp yellow teeth.

"Sure," said Lorenz and handed her the match. Anna lit the explosive.

With a loud bang the chickens were shot up to the sky. Several more Rottweilers leapt to it, grabbed onto it and chewed on it while descending rapidly.

Sam thought it was beautiful, like a Rottweiler air show. Except the beautiful moment didn't last long.

The Rottweilers, the meat and the dogs holding onto the meat all disappeared out of sight, crashing to the ground.

Sam watched the remaining bloody Rottweilers, greedily. The smell of blood made him ravenous. He wanted a chance to fight them with his own fangs, but nearly all the Rottweilers had leapt to their death down below.

He could wait no longer. The moment had come, he realized. It was his opportunity to make a contribution to the battle.

He climbed to the top of the castle roof, and stood atop the railing. Feeling his vampire power, Sam jumped toward the remaining Rottweilers still clinging to the castle wall.

His family on the roof top was dumbfounded and deeply alarmed as he plummeted past them. "Sam!" Their screams followed him.

"I'm fine," he called back, descending slowly. His cape now had become giant wings. Then he heard a voice.

"Sam, we're coming to help you!"

He looked back and saw six bats flying toward him. When they came closer, he recognized them. They were his parents, his aunt and uncle, and Grandpa and Grandma. With their support, he felt more confident.

He glided slowly toward the wall and the dogs, grabbing one and chewing it to death. He grabbed another, and another, until all the attacking canines were dead.

Morning had come. Sam opened his eyes and saw Max, snoring in the bed next to his. Sunlight streaked through the thin curtain. He sat up, thinking he'd just had a scary dream, rather Halloweenish. It was surely a dream, right? His mind cleared and he recollected the haunted castle, the bees Max found, and the vicious Rottweilers. He could still feel the sensation of gliding in the sky, a little scared but having so much fun. He had never felt so free. Then he remembered eating the vicious Rottweilers.

He thought could still taste the blood in his mouth, but his hands were warm, and he had no fangs.

"Breakfast is ready!" Sam could hear his mother's voice from below.

He tried to wake Max, gently pushing him. "Wake up. Breakfast is ready. Can't you smell the bacon and eggs?"

"Yum." It looked like Max was still enjoying the honey in his dream.

Sam decided to go down stairs alone. He was hungry and decided Max would come down as soon as he smelled the food.

He was right. Max arrived in pajamas as soon as Sam sat down.

Everyone, all twelve of them, kids and adults sat around the table.

Two big pans of egg bake were served, which was Sam's favorite breakfast along with the freshly squeezed orange juice, a California specialty, but a rarity in Bavaria. It was served because the owners, Wilhelm and Peggy, spent most of their time in their southern California home.

After breakfast, instead of going back to her books, Chloe asked Anna to help her practice a piano piece to perform that evening in the ballroom. Lorenz and Stefan went outside to practice fencing, and Max asked Sam to practice archery with him.

No one mentioned the night before.

Sam was determined to appreciate the remaining one week there. The castle was fun and despite what his cousins had said, certainly not boring at all.

ROSE
By Shaun Allan

"When the dark winds blow
When dark things prey
When the shadows walk
When all things Fey
Become the night
And forget the day
I'll come for you
And take you away."

"You said it wrong!" the girl said.

"What do you mean? I said it right!"

"No, you didn't. You said it all wrong! It's not 'fey', it's 'lay'!"

"What?" The boy pushed his sister, causing her to fall against the cabinet she'd only a second before been leaning against.

"What was that for?" she cried.

"'When all things Fey'? What's 'fey'?? There's no such thing!" Adam, the boy, shouted. His sister, Sarah, tried to pull herself up, attempting to do so without touching any of the dusty, web-covered furniture scattered about the attic. She'd almost managed to stand when he pushed her again.

"Ow! Adam! What was that for?"

"Because you're a numpty. You've spoiled it now. Everyone knows you can only do spells once or they don't work."

"Who says so? There's no rules for spells, that's ridiculous!"

"Of course there are. Everyone knows that."

Sarah stuck her tongue out. "You're making that up."

"Am not," insisted her brother. "And don't put that tongue back in your mouth. It's dirty!"

Sarah giggled and Adam couldn't help but smile.

"Come on," he said, putting the old book back in the drawer they'd removed it from. "Let's go play hide and seek in the woods."

"You know I don't like it in there. Mum said I don't have to go in and you're not allowed to make me."

"Hey, that's fine," said Adam, smiling. He brushed the dust off his jeans and slapped his hands together to shake them clean. "I'm not making you do anything you don't want to. I wouldn't do that. You're the eldest so you're the boss. That's what Mum says. I'm going to go, though. If you want to stay up here with the spiders and rats, be my guest."

Sarah looked around, biting her bottom lip. She knew there were no rats. Their dad had made sure when they'd moved in three weeks previously. Spiders were another matter, though. Webs seemed to cling to everything, intent on trapping the siblings and holding them tight for the spiders to come and feast upon their paralysed bodies...

She shook her head.

"No, it's fine. If you really can't play without me, I suppose I'll come. Wouldn't want you to get scared."

Adam smiled. He knew his sister well, and the hint of spiders or anything larger would be too much for her. She said she wasn't scared of them—they just made her uncomfortable—but she'd still scream if one touched her or if she walked through a cobweb. If the latter happened, Sarah would suddenly become like the puppet of a madman, arms flailing wildly as she tried to brush away the webs and any attached creepy crawlies.

"Thanks, Sis," he said. "I knew you'd keep me safe."

"Always," she said.

"Come on then, freak."

Adam scrambled to the opening in the floor and clambered down the ladder onto the upper landing of their home. He held it as his sister climbed down after him.

"I suppose Tom will have to come with us?" Sarah asked, the hope that the answer would be "no" apparent in her voice.

"Sorry, Sis. You know he'll moan and Mum will insist."

"Yeah," sighed Sarah. "Never mind. He can be 'It.'"

"Suits me."

The pair ran downstairs and through the kitchen into the back garden. Their mother, Amanda, stood at the sink, peeling potatoes.

"What are you two up to?" she asked suspiciously. She was always wary when her older children were getting on. It usually meant mischief. Though she wouldn't admit it out loud, it was more comforting to have them bickering. At least then they were more or less behaving.

"Nothing, Mum," they replied in unison.

Sure, she thought. *I believe you.*

"What are you doing now? Dinner will be ready in an hour or so."

"Can we go play hide and seek in the woods?" asked Sarah. They knew if she asked the answer was more likely to be "yes." Their parents seemed to automatically assume Adam would be doing something he shouldn't be, whereas Sarah was "exploring her boundaries," as the adults put it. Adam used to hate the favouritism, but soon learned to use it to his advantage with the cooperation of his sister.

"I'd rather you didn't, guys," Amanda said. "Dinner will be ready soon."

"Not for an hour, Mum." said Sarah.

Adam nodded. "We'll take Tom with us."

Tom was their youngest brother, five years Adam's junior, while there was a year separating him from Sarah. He would often be in Adam's shadow, following him around like a pet dog who was pleased to see its owner home from work for the day. It was tiring for the older boy, but he did like having a baby brother.

"Well...I suppose so." The two children cheered as their mother continued, "Make sure you stay near the house. I don't want to have to come looking for you once dinner is done."

"OK, Mum," said Sarah. "We will."

Adam ran back into the house and was followed a moment later by Tom. They careened past their sister who laughed and ran with them, disappearing into the trees that lined the back of their house.

"Don't go too far!" Amanda shouted, following them out into the garden. "Listen out for dinner!"

She heard her children yell something back at her but couldn't make out what. It didn't matter. They were having fun, and they'd soon be back for their meal when they smelled the food and their stomachs reminded them of their mother's instructions. She turned to walk back into the house, but a noise stopped her. It was low and rumbling—either quiet or distant, she couldn't tell. She looked up to see if an airplane was flying overhead. The sky was clear, almost cloudless. She looked over to the tree line but saw nothing. Her children had disappeared. She listened intently then smiled with relief as she heard their laughter.

The potatoes wouldn't peel themselves, she thought. Her own stomach grumbled at the thought of food, and she returned to the kitchen sink to prepare the meal.

The house was old, a huge structure which had been added to over the decades by various owners. It had become a mismatched building which looked thrown together. It was as if a child had been using oversized building blocks one rainy afternoon and had created a haphazard jumble of rooms before becoming bored and turning to colouring or the television. The oddly misshaped aspect of the house was part of its charm, as far as Amanda and her husband Ian were concerned. It was what drew them to it.

The endless acres of forest at the back only added to the attraction. There were (though the family had yet to see them), deer, rabbits, and foxes residing amid the trees. In winter, they would supposedly be able to choose a Christmas tree from the many hundreds hiding therein. It was too good to pass up. They knew the previous owners had died in the house some time before they bought it and they felt guilty that it pushed down the asking price, but they instantly fell in love when they saw it.

It was as if the house was the home they'd always searched for.

Her husband, Ian, was at work. He'd opened a printing business in the town and was being kept busy—sometimes too busy. But he had to make a name for himself and busy meant savings and holidays and food. Busy was sometimes lonely, but it was good in the long run.

Amanda picked up a potato and began to scrape it with the peeler. She hummed softly to herself.

"If you go down to the woods today..."

Sarah, Adam, and Tom were enjoying themselves in their new home. The forest was full of places to hide and trees to climb. Today was really the first time the children had properly been able to explore, and they were relishing the moment, even including Tom in their play. Granted, he was "It" and he was struggling to find them, but that was part of the game and part of the fun.

As they ran and hid and jumped on top of each other, they moved deeper into the forest. It was fine, though, she thought. They'd still be able to hear their mum. She had a loud voice, especially when she was shouting at her children. Besides, Sarah had her watch on. She would know when an hour had passed.

Adam was concealed behind his brother, pressed against the trunk of a large oak. He could see Sarah over to his left, hidden. He waved to her and she returned the gesture, smiling. Tom ran about from tree to bush to tree. His laugh was infectious, and both siblings had to hold their hands over their mouths to stifle their own sniggers.

"Come on out!" he shouted. "I can't find you!"

Adam put his arms to his side, making himself as thin as possible, and Sarah ducked down further, tucking her legs under her body and wrapping her arms around herself. Tom was coming closer, and the anticipation threatened to burst out of them, declaring their hiding places in fits of giggles.

"Adam! Sarah! I don't want to play anymore!"

Typical Tom. If he couldn't find you immediately, he became bored and started moaning. Adam saw Sarah look at him, her gaze questioning. She was asking him if they should come out, reveal their location to keep their little brother happy. He shook his head.

Not this time. Sarah shrugged and then nodded. She knew Adam was right. Tom needed to learn. He gave in too easily and spent the rest of the day whining. This time he could play the game properly and find them. He just needed to look, that was all. There were only so many hiding places, even in a forest this big. Look behind the trees. Delve into the bushes. Peek over the decaying, fallen sections of trunk.

Adam held his breath as he heard his brother shuffling about. The energy had left his gait, and he was now moping. Well, tough. Tom wouldn't like it if Adam or Sarah went mardy and moaned all the time. He could find them, that was it. Adam himself was growing tired of hide and seek anyway. He wanted to climb and explore. He wanted to find hidden treasures or get scratches and scrapes from trying. Tom was getting in the way of that.

Sarah would join in—she wasn't what their father called a "girlie girl." She enjoyed the same things as he did, which was one of the reasons they got on so well. The fact she hated spiders simply gave him some ammunition. It didn't stop her climbing into dusty old lofts or falling-down garages. It just meant he could scare her once she did.

He heard Tom stop moving. The boy was fairly close to the tree his brother was hiding behind. Adam desperately wanted to peer out but knew Tom could be looking in his direction and the game would be up.

He heard Tom yelp, a part cry, part choke which was followed by a deep growl he could feel through the bark of the tree trunk.

Then Tom screamed.

The growl became a snapping snarl, and Adam felt a thud as something very large landed heavily nearby.

He began to shake, fear replacing the excitement he'd been feeling. He looked over at Sarah and saw she was shaking too. He could see tears beginning to fall down her cheeks. He moved to look around the tree, but Sarah shook her head. No! Stay where you are!

There was a crunch, and Tom's scream was cut off. Adam couldn't help himself—he had to look. Slowly, he eased himself away from the tree and moved his head so he could just see what was happening.

At first, he couldn't make out what he was seeing. It was a large mass of black and grey fur with thick legs holding up a huge body. He gasped when he realised what it was.

Wolf!

The animal looked around at the sound. An arm, Tom's arm, was hanging from its mouth. Blood streaked the maw and dripped from the fingers of the hand. Adam could see his brother's head. It had been torn from his body and lay, dead eyes staring, at the wolf's feet.

The beast stared at Adam then picked up the head in its mouth. It looked back at the boy before snapping down, teeth popping through the bone to crush Tom's head. Brain and blood splattered the ground. A piece of skull fell at Adam's feet.

Sarah screamed, and the wolf turned, calmly, in her direction. It didn't need to rush or be fearful. It seemed to know if they ran, it would catch them. If Tom was dinner, they would be dessert. It snarled at the girl, baring its teeth. Red eyes stared for a moment, then the wolf turned and continued to feast on its kill.

Adam and Sarah looked at each other, terror apparent on both their faces. Adam then ran at his sister, grabbed her hand and, dragging her along behind him, ran deeper into the forest.

The wolf looked up and watched them go. It growled, briefly, then returned to its meal.

Sarah's breath was burning in her chest. It felt she'd been running so long and so fast, the air was all behind her and all that was left was an invisible fire she was forced to breathe in as they went.

"St...stop!" she panted, pulling her hand from her brother's grip. She stumbled and fell forward, barely missing a thick root snaking across the mud from the base of the nearest tree. Adam carried on a few more paces then stopped too.

"What are you doing?" he said, his own breath ragged. "We can't stay here! You saw what that thing did to Tom! We have to keep moving!"

"But we don't know where we're going, Adam!" she said, pushing herself up to a crouch. "We're just running. I don't know which direction the house is, and if Mum shouts, we won't be able to hear her!" She paused, her hand to her mouth. "What if Mum shouts and it gets her too?"

Adam didn't know what to say. He was the male. He was meant to be strong and was often the leader of their little group, but this time he was terrified. He was straining not to pee himself out of fear and not to cry in front of his sister. She had no such restrictions. Tears started to fall freely, and he saw a puddle of urine begin to spread at her feet. She looked horrified, and he wasn't sure whether it was because of the pee or the wolf. He ignored it, either way.

"It won't. It will be chasing us. That's why we can't stay here."

"But you don't know that. It already ate... ate... T..." Sarah couldn't finish the sentence. Sobs broke up the words into fractured emotions, and she buried her head in her arms.

Adam looked around, worried about where the wolf was. He couldn't hear it, but that didn't mean it wasn't close. He couldn't think about Tom, not yet. He couldn't end up sobbing like his sister. He had to keep them moving. Maybe they could circle round and make it back to their house. They'd call the police. The police would help. They'd know what to do.

Adam took his sister by the arms and pulled her to her feet.

"We need to go, Sarah," he said, softly. "Now."

"But..."

"Now, Sarah."

The girl nodded, wiping her tears and snot away on her sleeve. This was something she'd not done since she was three years old. She felt something like that now.

"Can you run?" Adam asked.

Sarah nodded, sniffing. She knew she had to, though she also felt as if her feet were glued to the forest floor.

"Come on then, let's go!"

As they set off again, they heard the wolf's howl behind them. It was too close. Too loud. Too hungry. They found renewed energy and ran faster. With no direction in mind apart from away from the animal, the siblings could only run blindly. There were no paths this deep into the woods, and the trees grew randomly with roots spreading in all directions, threatening to trip them if they lost concentration. Both brother and sister kept their eyes firmly on their course, haphazard though it was.

A howl, to their right. A dart to their left. Crunching twigs. Thudding paws. With every sound, they changed their direction to move away. The children had no idea if the noises were from the wolf, but they had no choice but to try and avoid it. Their strength was flagging, however, and the closer the sounds came, the heavier their feet seemed to become.

"Look!" panted Sarah. She was pointing ahead. "A light! Is that... Is that smoke?"

Adam looked to where she was indicating, and a sense of hope burned away the tiredness.

"A house!"

"Is it ours?"

"I don't think so, Sis. But who cares? Let's just get there!"

The pair held hands, gaining a boost from the contact, and pushed on towards the building. As they grew nearer, the trees thinned and then stopped, creating a clearing around the house which was covered in myriad flowers and plants, none of which the children recognised. They could still hear the crashing of the wolf through the forest as they entered the clearing, and the sudden absence of trees made them feel uncomfortably exposed.

Running up to the front door of the house, they hammered at the aged wood. The paint had long since peeled away, and the remaining surface was weather-worn and tired. It shook and banged against its frame, looking as if it could shake loose at any moment.

No one answered for a long moment, and the children turned to face the forest, despair making them tremble as the red eyes of the wolf stared at them from the shadow of the trees' canopy. It howled, a triumphant yell telling the siblings they were out of luck. They were lunch. They were dead.

Then the door opened, and the pair fell backwards into darkness. A hand grabbed each of them, stopping them from hitting the ground.

"What's going on here? What's all the noise for?" The voice sounded ancient and dry, as if paper, kept for centuries in an old locked box, had suddenly found a way to speak.

Adam and Sarah spun and began to babble together, talking over each other in a rapid stream of words which threatened to drown them both. The hands which had held them went up, telling them to stop. A woman stepped into the light from the open door. She was tall, impossibly thin, impossibly old, and yet still stunningly beautiful. The children stopped abruptly. The woman crouched down to speak to them, and they still found they had to look up to make eye contact.

"What's going on? Who are you children? Why are you here?"

At first they couldn't answer. Relief had seemed to dry up their mouths, and exhaustion had swept the words away. The woman raised an eyebrow quizzically, and the words began to flow again, this time calmer. Still, both children were speaking, and a hand was raised once more.

"One at a time, please. I can't be doing with all this noise. You, boy. What's your name?"

Adam took a deep breath and told her.

"Adam. That's a good name. Strong. I like it. Now, girl. Who are you?"

"I'm Sarah," she said. "But you've got to close the door! There's a wolf out there! It killed our brother! It *ate* him!"

The tears and sobs she'd held at bay during the remainder of their flight pushed their way to the surface, and she struggled to keep them from bursting forth.

"Whoa now. Slow down. Sarah. Another good name." The woman took their hands and held them tight. It made them feel strangely safe, as if they were now protected, and no savage beast could hurt them. "What's all this about a wolf? And your brother?"

It was Sarah's turn to take a deep breath. She couldn't help the tears from falling but did her best to ignore them.

"Tom, our brother. We were playing. A wolf attacked us. It ate Tom, and we ran away. We left our brother."

"Child, what could you do?" The woman put her long arm around Sarah and pulled her close. She smelled of fresh-cut grass. "If you'd stayed, that horrid beast could have taken you too. You did what you had to."

Sarah buried her head in the woman's embrace and let the pain flow. The woman held her tightly without speaking. She looked at Adam, who could only stare at his sister. He wanted to be in there, wrapped in the woman's arms, letting his hurt and loss out. He stayed where he was and returned her gaze. She nodded to him and held out her free arm. He hesitated then joined Sarah.

It seemed long moments before the woman let them go and stood again. The children felt lighter, as if she had taken their pain from them, leaving them with a sense of loss but not one of hurt.

"Now," she said, finally. "What of this wolf?"

Adam and Sarah glanced at each other. They had almost forgotten about the animal which had torn their brother apart.

"Don't worry," said the woman. "It can't get you in here. You're perfectly safe.

"But your door?" said Adam. "I could have broken it with my fist! If it's hunting us, it can easily get in here and... and *kill* us! And you too!"

"Don't underestimate an old woman." Her parchment voice crackled in the dim light. The children fancied they could see sparkles in the air with each word. "I've lived here for a long time. I'm still here, now. So, tell me."

"It was a wolf," said Adam, "but it seemed bigger, angrier. Well, I don't know how angry wolves are, but this one seemed to be just vicious. But it's size... It was like three wolves in one!"

"And where is it now?"

As one, the children pointed towards the door.

"We ran, but it followed us," said Sarah. "I think it's still out there now."

The woman sighed and ran her hands through her silvering hair.

"So, it's trespassing on my property? We'll see about that." She stooped down so she was at eye level with the children. "Stay in here, you hear? And don't look out. I don't want it to see you're in here. Got it?"

The children nodded.

"Good. I'll be back before you know it."

The woman turned her back on them and pulled a long coat from a stand by the door. It was black and looked dusty. She wrapped it close around her and walked out of the door, closing it behind her.

Adam and Sarah moved closer together and held each other tightly. It didn't seem as comforting as it had when the woman held them, but it was all they had. Unconsciously, they stepped away from the door, taking refuge in the twilight within the room. They remained silent, thinking the slightest noise could alert the animal to their presence. They could feel each other shaking and pulled themselves closer together.

Outside, the woman walked calmly to the edge of the clearing. She looked straight ahead, listening. She could hear the wolf, though wolf was only a small part of what the animal truly was, breathing nearby. It was trying to keep its breaths low and even and hidden, but her ears were sensitive. They belied the longevity of her years, which had advanced much further than her appearance, old though she seemed, suggested.

"Come out," she said.

The wolf didn't move from its concealment. It watched her, eyes trained on her slender form.

"I said, come out." Her voice was composed but had an imperative undertone. She wasn't asking; she was telling. The animal realised this. It crept forward and stood in front of the woman. Even though she was tall, the beast towered over her. She looked up at its face.

"Don't make me repeat myself again," she said. "You know what will happen."

"Sorry, my lady," said the wolf. Its voice was a rumble of distant thunder, and she could feel it vibrate through her. "I meant no disrespect."

"Yes," she said. "Disrespect is exactly what you meant. It is becoming a habit. Once more and you will find yourself with another inside of you. Perhaps a snake this time. Snakes are lowly, prostrate creatures and I believe you would benefit from some humility."

"Please, my lady, you promised no more! I struggle with the burden of the ones I carry. You said the wolf would be the last!"

"Yes, I did, didn't I? Well, I don't even listen to myself, so why should you?"

The wolf bowed its head. It had served the witch for a century, having been born a hound but having been transformed with each mutation. She captured a creature, slaughtered it by moonlight and, with a touch of her finger and a muttered spell, combined the dead with the living. It was a horrifically painful spell which made her pet feel a continuous, tortured agony, but, as her familiar, it was unable to do anything but accept. Its form changed to become a sickening version of whatever new animal the witch had chosen, but all that had gone before served to ensure its form would forever be deviant.

"My lady."

"So. Why the two children? They tell me there was a third. Younger, I believe. Prime. Yet, you ate it?"

The wolf growled, but this time it was one of supplication. "I thought..."

"You thought? You *THOUGHT*?"

"Lady..." the wolf laid its head down on its forelegs. "I wanted to make sure they came this way! Killing their brother scared them into flight!"

"As would a howl, a growl and a snap of those teeth! You didn't need to kill one! I could have made use of him!"

"I'm sorry, my lady. I thought I was doing what was best."

The witch raised her hand, and the wolf flinched.

"I decide what is best. You do only what I decide. *Do* you understand?"

"Yes, my lady. I understand. It won't happen again."

"No. It won't."

She touched the wolf's nose with her finger and said three words under her breath. The wolf, for that was its current, most recognisable form, whimpered. The burning began deep within its body, near its heart. As its blood began to boil, searing through its veins, the whimper became a snarl. It wanted to attack the witch, to do to her what it had done to the boy. It wanted to, but it couldn't. The wolf was in her thrall, and through the melting of it's insides, it could only look at her. And hate her.

The witch watched her creation. If she was capable of such a feeling, she might have been sad. However, sadness was something only those with hearts themselves could experience. The witch had removed hers long ago. It was stored in a locked box behind the fireplace in her house. Close enough for her to feel its beat, but with an eternally lit fire, beyond her reach. She smiled as blood oozed and popped from the wolf's orifices and licked her lips when the ochre liquid splashed her mouth. The snarl diminished to become the whimper once more, then stopped. The parts of the creature's anatomy which could make such sounds had melted. An eye fell from its socket, hanging from the optic nerve before that, too, dissolved. The eye hit the ground and melted away, steaming.

The witch turned and walked back to the house. She didn't look back. By the time she had closed the door behind herself, the wolf was gone. A pus-like fluid soaked into the earth, leaving a wet patch which dried quickly. The grass, yellow from heat and acidity, was the only remaining indication of the wolf's existence.

Adam and Sarah threw themselves at the woman. They clung to her as if she was their mother, and she held them as if they were her children.

"It's ok," she said softly. "It's not out there. It must have gone."

"Are you sure?" asked Sarah.

"I'm sure," said the witch. "You're safe now."

The witch pulled herself free of the siblings and stepped back. She smiled at them warmly.

"Let's get you something to eat," she said. "You must be starving. Look at you both, there's nothing on you!"

Sarah's hand went to her mouth. Dinner! Their mother was going to shout them! Had it been an hour? It couldn't have been, not yet. They would have to tell her what had happened. They'd have to go home but...what if the wolf was still out there? She told this to the woman.

"Don't fret. I'm sure it's gone, but if you're concerned, stay here, eat, and I'll let your mother know you're safe."

"But she'll be worried," said Adam. "We should go, really."

"Well, if you want to go back out there, be my guest," she said, indicating the door. "Or you can stay here, have some food, and I'll speak to your mother."

The children looked at each other, and Adam nodded. Sarah followed suit and they smiled at the woman.

"Excellent. Now, the bathroom is through there, so go wash up and I'll sort out something to eat. I like pie. How does that sound?"

At the mere mention of food, Adam's stomach seemed to remember it needed sustenance and grumbled its assent.

"Yes, please," he said.

"Good. I'll get it on. Won't be long as I have it all prepared."

The children looked at each other as they walked to the bathroom and frowned. How could she have it already prepared? Another thought occurred to Sarah.

"We haven't told you our number to call Mum," she said.

"True," said the woman. "Where do you live?"

"Erm... We live on the edge of the forest. It's a big, funny-looking house."

"Yes," said Adam. "It's got bits sticking out all over."

"I know the one. I used to live there a long time ago."

"You did?" exclaimed Sarah. "When?"

"Oh, so long ago. Way before you were born. I'm sure it's been added to since then. It was a marvellous misshape when I lived there."

"Why did you leave and come here?"

The woman sighed and looked down. She smoothed her dress down with her hands and picked an invisible thread from her sleeve.

"I needed some solitude," she said. "I...didn't get on with my neighbours." She smiled broadly, adding, "I much prefer it here. Nobody bothers me. In fact, I think I've even been forgotten about, which suits me just fine."

Adam and Sarah couldn't imagine why anyone would want to live alone in the depths of a forest nor why they'd be happy to be forgotten, but the fact the woman had once lived in their house almost made them family, after a fashion. The pair smiled and turned back to the bathroom.

"Oh," said Adam, pausing. "What's your name?"

The witch smiled again. "Call me Rose," she said. "My real name is much longer than that, but you can call me Rose."

"Rose," said Sarah. "I like that name. It's our mum's favourite flower."

And I'm now going to be her thorn, thought the witch. She entered the kitchen and fired up the massive oven. She pulled down the door to watch the long flames lick the inside and licked her own lips. After a deep breath, she busied herself with vegetables and potatoes.

"You're not going to peel yourselves," she said quietly. "At least, not with those children here. Can't have them seeing that..."

She gave Adam and Sarah plates and cutlery and asked them to set the table. It wasn't long before the meal was ready and they were all seated.

"Did you speak to our mum?" asked Adam. He took a bite out of the pie, succulent steak and gravy filling his mouth. He couldn't help but moan in pleasure. He couldn't remember ever having eaten anything as delicious.

"Is that good?" Rose asked.

Sarah was similarly chewing and moaned herself. The pie was perfection in a mouthful. Both children went to respond, intending an animated nodding, but found they couldn't move their heads. Or their hands. Or...

Paralysed, Adam and Sarah could only stare straight ahead. The witch pushed her finger into each of their mouths, extracting the half-eaten food.

"I don't want you choking, do I? That would be no good at all. Not at all."

She whispered something and touched their foreheads.

"There," she said. "You can look around now—or at least move your eyes. I wouldn't normally allow that, but I must be getting soft in my old age. A century ago, you'd have no chance. I might even have blinded you."

From where the siblings were sitting, they could see each other if they looked out of the corners of their eyes. The witch pulled their chairs around so they were facing each other.

"Better?" she asked. She paused, but neither child was able to utter a sound. She began to pace around the table, talking to the air but directing her comments at her prisoners. "Ignore me then. It's fine. I don't expect thanks, not from children. You're all the same. Selfish. Ignorant. Not interested in the thoughts and feelings of others. I'm used to it. Oh well, we'll soon change that, won't we?"

She lifted a large bowl from the corner of the room and carefully placed it in the centre of the table. It was filled with a dark liquid that seemed to slide rather than move freely as water might.

"This, my sweets, is the blood of all the silly, awful children who have passed by over the years. So many."

She dipped her finger into the bowl and then sucked it.

"See? It even tastes bitter."

She moved in front of Adam and crouched down. Sarah couldn't see past the witch's head to see what she was doing. Desperately she tried to scream, but her chest felt frozen and her mouth was numb. The witch stood and moved away from the girl's brother. She had something in her hands, and Sarah watched her to see what it was. The witch turned to face the table and plunged her hands into the blood, giving Sarah a fleeting glimpse of... what...? Was it...?

Her eyes whipped back to her brother. She wanted to cry out. She needed to vomit. She needed to empty her bowels and her bladder. Adam stared back at her, terror in his eyes. He couldn't see his body, but he had seen what Rose had lifted away from him. Though she wished she could close her eyes, Sarah could see her brother's body very well. It had been cut from the neck down past his navel. The skin had been peeled back, and the rib cage removed to be balanced on his knees.

There was a gap where his right lung should have been.

The witch was humming to herself. She took the removed lung back to the boy and pushed it back into place, whispering something as she did. The lung reattached itself to Adam's innards, and his heart dropped out into Rose's hand. She returned to the bowl of blood and repeated the submersion and reinsertion into his chest.

Methodically, she removed each organ in turn, including the intestines, which trailed along the floor as the witch walked, thrust it into the bowl and replaced it in Adam's torso. When she was finished, she picked up his ribcage, held it in place and muttered a spell. Sarah could hear the bones crack and snap as they joined back together. The skin was next, Rose folding it back and running her finger up the joint to melt it back together.

She walked behind Adam and placed her hands on his head. After speaking her enchantment, she made a slight twisting motion and lifted off the top of his skull. Sarah would have fainted if she'd been able to. The witch reached in and removed the brain. She stood for a moment with it in her hands, examining it. She brought it to her face and sniffed and then made to lick its surface, though stopped short.

"No," she said to herself. "Don't do that. You'll spoil it. It does smell delectable, though."

She took the brain to the bowl of blood and immersed it, chanted her spell and dropped it back into the cavity of Adam's head. Carefully replacing the section of skull, Rose clapped her hands together.

"All done," she said. "Now for you, missy. You won't feel a thing, I promise."

Sarah's eyes were so wide they bulged as the witch approached her. She could do nothing, however, as Rose repeated her disembowelling ritual. Adam looked on, equally helpless, watching his sister being taken apart piece by living piece. Once she was finished, Rose looked at them both, smiling broadly.

"All done!" she said. "See how easy that was? And you managed to behave yourselves for all that time. There's hope for you yet!"

"What's that? You have a question?" she asked, leaning towards Sarah, touching her forehead.

Sarah suddenly found she could move her head and her mouth. She opened it and let out a piercing scream which made her brother wince. Rose was unmoved. She touched Sarah's head once more, causing it to freeze, the mouth contorted into the now silent shriek.

"Now, now. I give you a chance and that's how you repay me. Just the same as all the rest." The witch crouched down between the children and smiled. "It will be all right now. One little spell and you can be on your way. I've washed all your nastiness and cruelty away in the blood of the boys and girls who have paid me visits. It means I've made you kind and good and the sort of children who won't ridicule or push or provoke poor ladies who can't defend themselves."

She stood and reached out, laying a hand on each of their heads. She closed her eyes and started to speak:

"When the dark winds blow
When dark things prey
When the shadows..."

She paused and opened her eyes, looking around.

"Something's wrong. The blood should be boiling. You two should be glowing."

The witch walked over to the bowl and dipped her finger in.

"Well, it's warm," she said. "Not quite what I expected. Oh well." She turned to Adam and Sarah. "I have to be careful, you know. A spell can only be said once, and it has to be said right or anything can happen. I've waited a long, long time to do this. It's got to be right first time."

She returned to her spot between them and rested her hands on their heads again.

"Try again," she said, closing her eyes.

"When the dark winds blow
When dark things pray
When the shadows walk
When all things Fey
Become the night
And forget the day
I'll come for you
And take you away"

When she was finished, the witch lowered her hands and opened her eyes. The bowl of blood had begun to bubble and steam. A faint glow was surrounding each child. She clapped her hands triumphantly.

"It's working! Now you are all nice and normal, and you can bring me lots of other children to cleanse!"

She touched the children in turn, releasing them from their paralysis. They dropped to their knees, their bodies momentarily forgetting how to control themselves. Adam and Sarah stared at each other from eyes rapidly turning red. They could feel their bodies changing. Fingers became claws. Teeth elongated and sharpened. Spines split through the skin, barbs appearing along the vertebrae. Tongues became forked and limbs thickened.

Rose backed away, horror masking her face. She hit the table and stopped, unable to go further.

"What's happening? What's gone wrong? It should have worked!"

Sarah looked up at the witch and smiled, a snarling twist of her mouth.

"The spell has already been used!" she hissed.

"What? How? Impossible!"

It was Adam's turn to smile, his being a vicious rupture of hate.

"You shouldn't leave your old books lying around in attics, witch!"

Rose gasped. She would have spoken, questioning, invoking, insisting, but the children, or whatever they were becoming, leapt on her. Her throat was torn out, her head crushed. Her stomach had been ripped apart.

When they had finished and the witch was no longer twitching, Adam and Sarah left, the door splintering as they crashed through it. They lifted their heads to smell the breeze and then loped off into the forest. They had children to find.

Children to feast upon.

HIDDEN
By Carlie M A Cullen

No, no, NO! This can't be happening – not again! His mind screamed as he heard noises on the front porch. Scuttling through the house with haste, he reached the in-house out-house, peeked down, and saw two young women with large rucksacks standing there. Rain had plastered their hair to their heads, and they looked like they'd been swimming fully clothed. The two were arguing, and he didn't have to strain his hearing.

"If we push on, we can make the next campsite in an hour. A bit of rain won't hurt us. C'mon, Caley, where's your sense of adventure?" the redhead wheedled.

"Being washed away along with every path around here!" Caley retorted as she removed the heavy-looking pack from her shoulders. She ran her fingers through her dripping blonde hair and pulled it off her face. "Be realistic for once in your life, Patricia. Look at that sky – does it seem like there's any chance this rain is going to stop soon? The temperature is beginning to drop and we're soaked through. I, for one, really don't fancy getting pneumonia. We can hole up here until the storm passes and then be on our way again. Assuming the owners don't mind, of course."

Pat knew when Caley used her full name, she meant business. "What if the owners aren't hospitable?"

"We'll ask if they have a shed or outbuilding we can bunk in. I really don't care as long as it's dry and protects us from the elements." Caley reached her hand up toward the door when Pat grabbed it.

"Hang on a minute. What if they haven't got an outbuilding? It *is* pretty isolated out here. What if they're like one of those families you see on horror films that are cannibals?"

"Oh, for god's sake! You're beginning to sound like my uber-annoying eight-year-old brother – what if, what if, what if." She parodied her friend's voice but made it sound much younger and childlike. "Don't worry, Pat, I'll protect you. But if you ask me, this place doesn't exactly look like the quintessential cannibal home. In fact, I would say this is well over one-hundred years old." Caley stepped back, almost to the edge of the veranda and stared at the cottage.

The stones used were rough-hewn and typical of the type of construction used by the poor over a century ago. With small, wood-framed windows, the cottage looked as if it would be quite gloomy inside – a good match for the current sky. The wooden veranda had been added later, but despite the peeling paint and weathered look, the treads under their feet felt as solid as if they'd recently been laid. Obviously good timber had been used.

Caley loved places like that and desperately wanted to own one. It was isolated, surrounded by trees, not too big, and not too far to the nearest town that she couldn't drive there for supplies. She glanced around the edges of the property. Wild flowers, once tall and standing proud, were now mostly lying flat, their stalks beaten into submission by the force of the precipitation. Primordial trees with huge trunks and thick branches encircled the cottage as if guarding it. In fact, the woods surrounding it were just as nature intended – unspoilt and unaffected by the ravages of man.

She stepped forward, and before Pat could stop her, she rapped on the door. They waited for a minute or two, but no one appeared. Caley knocked again, louder yet, still no response. She put her ear to the door but couldn't hear any sounds of habitation and then moved to peer through the grimy windows. Only vague shapes of what might be furniture could be seen. She tried the door and to her surprise found it unlocked. Opening it wide, she called out,

"Hello. Is anyone home?" With no answer forthcoming, Caley walked inside, with Pat reluctantly trailing behind her.

The furniture was covered in dust sheets, but to their surprise, the room was spotlessly clean.

"Well, this is unexpected," Pat said, pointing to the spotless floor. "Perhaps the owners have only just vacated the place." She pulled one of the dust sheets off with a flourish, and a massive cloud of particles flew into the air around them, making them cough and sneeze. "Weird. Shitloads of dust on the covers, but the rest of the place is pristine." Caley shrugged as she blew her nose.

Argh! All that dust over my nice, clean floor, he thought, annoyed, as he watched from his new vantage point. The girls dragged their heavy rucksacks in, trailing them through the dust and leaving horrible smudges. *Please don't let them stay. They mustn't stay. Not now when I'm so close.* The anguish filled his entire body, and a couple of stray tears leaked from his eyes. He continued to spy on them, keeping himself carefully hidden, as they stripped off their soaking outer garments.

"Thank god for water-resistant fabric," said Pat as she held her dripping coat at arm's length.

Caley looked at her and chuckled. "It's like someone has drawn a pen line around your clothes – the top half above the line is dry and the bottom is sodden." She removed her own coat and looked around for somewhere to hang it.

"You're a fine one to talk!" Pat pointed and giggled. Caley's were exactly the same. She watched as her friend squelched her way from room to room. Then she disappeared from sight.

"Hey! Back here!" she called out. Pat followed the sound and found Caley in a narrow room with a tiled floor. It had a large sink against one wall with a washboard on the counter next to it, an ancient mangle close by, and washing lines strung across the opposite side. Caley had already pegged up her coat and was in the process of removing her boots. She tipped them up over the sink, and a little trickle of water fell into the porcelain. Her socks and trousers came off next, and she put them through the mangle before hanging them up to dry. Pat followed suit, and as she returned to find some dry clothes in her pack, Caley grabbed a mop which stood in the corner and cleaned up the water by the mangle as best she could before returning to the lounge.

Standing there in her panties, t-shirt, and nothing else caused goose bumps on Caley's bare flesh. The temperature was still dropping outside and becoming unseasonably cold. She'd brought mainly shorts and strappy tops, expecting to be enjoying the warmth of the sunshine on her already tanned body, but luckily she'd had the sense to pack a couple of items in case the weather changed. She pulled out some trousers and socks and hurriedly put them on, followed by a thick cardigan.

Pat asked, only half-joking, "Well, now we're in the cannibals' lair, shall we have a quick nosey around before they come back and decide which bits of us they'll have for dinner?"

"Your trouble is you watch too many of those crappy, late-night, B-rated horror films! But yeah, I'm up for having a proper look around." Although Caley had peeked in the other couple of rooms downstairs, she hadn't really looked at anything.

Being nosey in other peoples' homes? Tsk. How dare they? I hope they don't wake it up! He scurried along, following them at a safe distance and making sure he moved as silently as possible.

The first room they came to was the kitchen. It had an outdated cooking range which ran on wood or coal, a pantry, and a counter running along the opposite wall to the cooker. A butcher's block sat on the worktop with a sharp, long-bladed knife sitting atop it. The blade itself was so spotless it looked brand new. Pat shuddered and was glad to follow Caley into the next room.

The small room was quite dark, the tiny window covered by low branches heavy with foliage and fruit. They could make out an old desk and chair against the wall where the window was. Squeezed into a corner a tall, thin cupboard stood, leaving just enough room for someone to slip between it and the desk. The top of the desk featured some faded papers. Pat walked over, picked them up, and scanned the text.

"Hey, look at these." A hint of disbelief coloured her tone.

Caley turned her head. "What is it?"

"This," she replied, passing the papers. "Loads of symbols and strange writing – it looks like spells to me."

Caley studied the documents. She recognised some of the symbols from research she'd carried out for an essay in her English class. "This is definitely something to do with witchcraft. And the writing has the cadence of a spell. I wonder what they're for. The heading is too faded and smudged to tell."

"From what little I read, it didn't sound like anything pleasant, that's for sure."

Oh no! Please don't let them read those aloud. I can't bear it! He watched from a gap between the door frame and the wall, shaking with fear. Relief poured through him as Caley placed the documents back on the desk a few minutes later.

"I have a bad feeling about these," she said as she put them down. "Let's go and explore the rest of the house."

As they moved toward the door, Pat turned her head back to the desk and suddenly let out a cry. She seemed transfixed by something and took on the appearance of a statue.

"Pat? What's the matter?"

Her voice was strained as she replied. "The chair... it moved on its own. It's like someone is sitting in it, watching us, listening to everything we say. There's evil in this room – I can feel it... a presence, malevolent, dark. We must *not* come back in here, no matter what we hear or see. The chair's just moved again and so have the papers. We have to go, *now*!" Pat rushed out the door and pulled Caley so hard they fell in a heap on the floor, a tangle of arms and legs.

"*Ouch*! What the bloody hell did you do that for?"

"I had to get you out, fast. It was coming for us." Pat's voice wavered, her face a mask of abject fear.

"What was?"

"I don't know. I couldn't see anything. I just felt the presence, and it was coming closer and closer. I've never felt anything so corrupt and evil, and it wanted us." Pat's voice rose as panic threatened to overwhelm her.

Caley extricated herself and stood, closing the door to the tiny room. "Right. Whatever's in there can stay behind that door, and we won't go in again, okay?"

Pat rose and nodded her head vigorously. "Okay," she replied in a small voice.

"Let's see what's upstairs. C'mon." Caley grabbed Pat's hand and led her up the creaky staircase to find three doors, all open. They walked in the nearest one and found an old-fashioned bathroom with a claw-footed tub, a sink, and a toilet. She turned on the hot tap and was surprised and delighted after a couple of minutes to feel warm water coming through. She wondered whether the stove was already lit and made a mental note to check. "Yay! We can have a bath." Pat smiled, the thought of a hot bath cheering her as she was beginning to get rather chilly.

They walked out of there and into the next room, finding a double bed and some old, solid-looking wooden furniture. Pat felt the mattress with her hand, and it was quite soft. Caley had opened the wardrobe door and was looking inside. On the rack was a selection of dated men's clothing. She shut the door and peeked into the top drawer of the dresser.

No! That's too much of an intrusion! he cried in his head as he looked down on them rifling through the drawers. *Really, some people need to learn respect for other peoples' belongings.* He was so incensed, he nearly tumbled out from his vantage point. Breathing a sigh of relief when she stopped nosing around, he scuttled after them as they went into the final room.

Finding a second bedroom, Pat clapped her hands with glee. This one was much smaller, although it still had a double bed with a soft mattress. A small dresser stood in one corner with a thin bookcase next to it. As she was an avid reader, she couldn't resist scouring the bookshelves and found several classics there which looked like first editions. She pulled one out and, opening it carefully, saw it was indeed a first edition Dickens. Holding the book with reverence, she gently flipped through a few pages before replacing it on the shelf.

"Trust you to find some books!" Caley said with mock exasperation. "I'm guessing you want this room then."

"Yeah, if that's okay with you?"

"Fine by me. Now, I think we ought to get a fire going downstairs and then have a warm bath before we catch a cold. Do you think you can tear yourself away from the books long enough to help me?"

"Oh, har, har. Of course I can. Let's go because I don't know about you, but I'm starting to feel really chilled."

"Yeah, I am too. That's why I made the suggestion," Caley threw over her shoulder as she left the room and began descending the stairs. Pat followed closely behind her. They approached the fireplace and were surprised to see everything for the fire had already been laid in the hearth – all they needed to do was light it. There was also a pile of logs next to the fireplace. "Weird!"

"What is?" Pat asked.

"To find an uninhabited house in the middle of the woods, which is very clean apart from what was on the dust covers, has a fire already laid and outdated men's clothes in the wardrobe. Do you think a ghost lives here?" Caley whispered the last conspiratorially.

"Don't start with all that! It's bad enough feeling that evil presence in the small room without you adding ghosts to the mix. I'm going to have enough trouble sleeping as it is."

"But don't you think it's a bit strange?" Caley persisted.

"Of course I do, but I hoped we might find a rational explanation." She pulled a lighter from her pocket, lit one of the long tapers lying there, and proceeded to light the fire. Within a few minutes, there was a roaring blaze in the fireplace and the girls were warm enough to take off their fleeces and Pat her hiking boots. Pat took the boots into the drying room where they'd hung their coats earlier, surprised to find it quite warm.

Caley had taken her pack upstairs and started running some bath water. Pat followed her up with her own rucksack and, laying it on the floor, unzipped it and pulled out her fleecy pyjamas, placing them on the coverlet of the bed. She wandered over to the small window and peered out. The sky was gunmetal grey and continued to spew forth copious amounts of rain. As she watched, lightning could be seen in the distance, and she had a feeling it wouldn't be too long before it reached them. A half-smile spread across her face. She loved thunderstorms, but Caley hated them. Perhaps it was time for a little payback after that comment about ghosts.

Pat turned away from the window, and her pyjamas were no longer on the bed. She automatically checked the floor, but there was no sign of them. Her forehead creased as she crouched by her rucksack. She opened it and there, neatly folded as they had been before, were her night clothes. *That's strange. I could have sworn I'd got them out a minute ago*, she thought as she laid them on the coverlet. She then pulled out a large towel and a small bag of toiletries, laying them on the bed also.

"Pat!" Caley's voice was tinged with worry.

"What's up?" she asked as she strode up to the bathroom door.

"I could have sworn I brought my towel in here, but it's gone. Can you check the bedroom for me, please?"

"Sure." Pat walked into the other room and found the still-folded towel on the bed. She picked it up and, after knocking on the bathroom door, marched in and put the towel where her friend could reach it. "Dipstick! You left it on the bed," she said, laughing.

"Honestly, I was sure I'd brought it in here." Caley laughed louder.

"How much longer are you going to be?"

"I'm about done. I just need to get out and dry off. Do you want me to start running your water while I finish off?"

"That would be great, yes please," Pat replied. "Give me a yell once you're out?"

"No worries. I won't be long at all, so you might as well start getting stripped off ready."

"Okay," Pat replied and walked back into her room. The bed was once more completely empty. Once she could put down to her imagination, but twice? No way. There was something going on here, and as much as the thought scared her, she determined to find out. She bent to her pack, and as before, the items had been neatly returned to their places. She pulled them out for a third time, laid them on the bed, and kept a close eye on them as she undressed. Leaving her trousers and socks on the bed, she had just wrapped the towel around her when Caley called out. Pat grabbed her washbag and padded into the now-empty bathroom.

Half an hour later, Pat emerged and walked into her bedroom. Her dry clothes, along with her pyjamas, were nowhere to be seen. "This is getting beyond a joke," she mumbled as she crouched beside her rucksack. Her nightclothes were back in the same place, and her dry clothes had been folded and placed inside. She grabbed her pj's and put them on then, holding her wet towel, descended the stairs. Walking into the drying room, she threw it over the line then walked into the lounge where Caley had thrown the dust sheets off the rest of the furniture and was lounging, wearing her pyjamas, in a large, padded, brown armchair, staring at the fire.

"Thanks for sorting out my clothes," Pat said.

"You're welcome," Caley replied absently then whipped her head round. "Er, what do you mean by sorting out your clothes?"

"Well, didn't you fold up my dry ones and put them in my rucksack?"

"No. Actually I was going to thank you for doing that with my dry stuff."

Pat paled. "I didn't."

"Oh! Well, who did then?"

"I don't know, but I think there's someone else in the house, and they're playing mind games with us. Three times I got my pj's out and put them on the bed, and each time they went missing and I found them folded and back in my rucksack. When I got out of the bath and saw my things were missing, I naturally assumed you'd folded them up for me."

"I laid my pyjamas on the bed before I went into the bathroom, and they were in my pack when I got out. I thought it was you folding up all my stuff and putting them away." Pat shook her head. "Okay, let's search the place from top to bottom and see what we can find." Caley rose and grabbed a poker from beside the fireplace. Pat grabbed another implement, and together they marched upstairs.

They searched the bathroom and both bedrooms, looking under the beds, checking for secret passages on the walls and at the back of the wardrobe, but found nothing. They then continued downstairs, checking every cupboard and possible hidey hole, avoiding the small study, and again turned up nothing.

"Perhaps the place is haunted," Pat said innocently, knowing her friend's feelings about ghosts.

"Don't even think it!" Caley snapped.

"Well, what other explanation is there?" Pat crossed her arms and stared at her friend.

"Maybe someone was hiding in that dreadful room."

"Well, *I'm* not going in there!" Pat retorted, fear apparent in her voice.

"Neither of us is. We can set a trap outside the door, then if anyone comes out, we'll know.

"I like that idea. What are you thinking of using?"

"Anything that will make a lot of noise in case it happens while we're in bed, but nothing breakable, maybe some saucepans from the kitchen. If we pile them up, it should work well," Caley explained.

"Okay, sounds good. Now in the meantime, my stomach thinks my throat's been cut. I'm going to sort out something to eat. I think we've still got some sandwiches left." Pat turned around to where they'd left the food bag, and it wasn't there. "Did you move the cooler bag?"

"No. We left it just inside the door, didn't we?"

"That's what I thought, but it's not there now. This is getting bloody ridiculous! Do you think someone's trying to tell us we're not wanted here?" Pat asked.

"Someone, or something, maybe. I've read about some old houses that take on a personality of their own and are able to manifest various happenings inside the walls."

"Ha! You? Read? That'll be a first!"

"Oh, har, har, har. Don't be a bitch. Just because I haven't got my nose stuck in a book every second of every day doesn't mean I don't read!" Caley retorted.

"Having a sense of humour failure now too? Tsk, Tsk." Pat laughed nervously.

"You're just trying to cover up the fact you're scared by diverting the conversation away and taking a cheap potshot at me. But if it's any consolation, I'm not exactly blasé about what's happening here. But we need to eat, so let's try and find the cooler bag, okay?"

Pat nodded her agreement. Caley had assessed the situation perfectly. She *was* scared, more than she cared to admit even to herself. She loved reading about the paranormal, both real life and fiction, but being in that situation herself wasn't her idea of fun.

They checked every room in the house, barring the one, and there was no sign of the cooler bag. On instinct, Pat opened the front door and found the bag on the porch. She picked it up and brought it inside.

"Found it. It was on the porch," Pat said anticipating her friend's question. "Perhaps we didn't bring it in like we thought."

"I could have sworn we did. Oh well, at least we've got it. Let's have a sandwich – I'm starving."

They took the bag through to the kitchen, and while Pat looked for some plates, Caley opened the bag and screamed. Pat rushed to her side immediately. "What's the matter?"

Caley didn't reply, just pointed at the bag. Pat looked in, and her stomach churned immediately. Inside were hundreds of maggots and bugs of all descriptions crawling and writhing like a moving carpet. Grabbing the bag by the handle and holding it away from her body, she carried it through the cottage, out to the porch, and set it down near the edge. Carefully she tipped the bag over and then upside down, whereby all the food tumbled out, but when she looked, there was no sign of the insects. She shook the bag then looked inside only to find it empty.

Pat knelt and began to gingerly pick up each of the food parcels, shaking them as she did so. All the maggots and other creatures had vanished as if they hadn't been there. She looked up to see Caley staring down with her eyes wide and her mouth agape. After collecting all the food and returning it to the cooler bag, Pat rose and joined Caley in staring down at the ground before taking her friend's arm and steering her back into the house.

Walking through to the kitchen, she pulled the sandwiches out of their wrappings and placed them on the clean plates she'd found. *Thank god all the food is well wrapped*, she thought, as she took the plates through to where Caley was sitting shivering. Pat set the plates on a small side table and crouched down beside her friend.

"Caley? It's okay now, love. You're not going mad – we both saw it. C'mon, hun, snap out of it." She rubbed Caley's arm as she spoke in soft tones. Her friend didn't move or respond in any way; it appeared she was in some sort of trance as she stared unseeing at the wall. Pat moved directly in front of her and spoke louder. "Caley!" Still nothing, so she grabbed her shoulders, shook her, and shouted, "CALEY!" Worry and fear in equal measure mingled in her voice.

Her eyes seemed to refocus, and Caley looked at Pat's worried face. "Why are you shaking me?" she asked, genuinely puzzled.

"You were in shock and had gone off to some lala land. It was the only way I could get through to you short of slapping you around the face. That was going to be my last resort. Are you okay, hun?"

Caley shook her head. "I'm not sure. I was seeing images of things that I think have happened in this house – terrible things, evil things. If there was another option for us for tonight, I wouldn't stay here."

Pat's legs were aching so she sat in the chair opposite, the food temporarily forgotten. "What sort of stuff did you see?"

"Séances, the devil, an orgy where animals were included, murders, a witch casting spells on people and turning them into dreadful creatures, monsters..." Caley shivered and stared down at the floor. "Look! You can see the outline of some symbols on the floor. They're not that clear, but you can just about see enough." She pointed, and Pat got on the floor to see. Sure enough, several markings were recognisable enough to be copied.

Pat rose and ran upstairs, reappearing with a notebook in her hand. She turned to the very back, got onto the floor, and began to copy what was etched there, eliciting Caley's help to move furniture where necessary. When she'd finished, she rose, grabbed a plate with sandwiches on, and began to eat. Between mouthfuls she said, "There's a pentagram in the centre of all the symbols, but I can't tell if it's upside down or not. I recognise a couple of them – they're to do with witchcraft. You see this one here?" She pointed as she showed it to Caley. "It's called a triquetra and this one...," her finger moved to a different drawing, "is a circle of life. One or two of the others look familiar to me, but I can't remember their names right now. I'll do some research when we get home. C'mon, eat your sandwich. It's fine, I promise."

"All right," Caley replied begrudgingly. She picked up the plate and examined every morsel until she was satisfied before any of it went near her mouth. She didn't blame Caley for being cautious, but the way she scrutinised the sandwiches almost made Pat burst out laughing despite her having done the very same thing. "What are we going to do if the weather is just as bad tomorrow?" Caley's voice was small, tremulous.

"Let's not worry about that until it happens," Pat replied, trying to sound unconcerned. She stood and took a few steps to the fire, adding another log. "Shall we see if we can get the stove working? We could make a cup of tea and perhaps even have something hot for supper. What do you think?"

"Sounds good to me." Caley rose and followed her friend into the kitchen. They found the stove had a pilot light on it; that would explain the presence of the hot water. As Pat lit one of the rings, Caley asked, "Have you ever used a stove like this before?"

"Not exactly the same, but my gran had something similar. I watched her more times than I can remember." As she replied, a heavy cloud of melancholy settled over her. It had been her gran's funeral just two weeks before they left for this trip. They'd always been really close, and her passing had been not only a massive shock but had pierced her to her core. The death had been sudden and unexpected, making it harder for her to come to terms with.

Her eyes started to prick, and before she could even try and stop them, tears rolled down her cheeks.

Caley pulled Pat into her arms and held her until she'd cried herself out. "Are you okay now, hun?" she asked in a gentle voice.

Pat blew her nose before replying. "Yeah. Sorry about that."

"You don't have to apologise, you silly moo. I know you're still grieving, and it's natural you're going to have these sorts of crying jags every so often. I'm just glad I can be here for you."

"You're a good friend, Caley. You've got such a kind heart. I don't know what I'd do without you."

Caley felt the heat rising in her cheeks. "Now look what you've done," she said playfully, pointing to her cheeks. Pat laughed, just as Caley had intended then changed the subject. "We'd better see if the water is okay to make tea with." She was fairly close to the sink so in two steps was able to turn the taps on. At first, the water was brown and gungy, but after a couple of minutes it began to clear. "Looks like tea is on the menu, so where was that kettle?" They opened a couple of cupboards and found it almost immediately. Pat carried the heavy, old-fashioned kettle to the sink where the water ran crystal clear, but as soon as she went to put the kettle under the tap, it changed colour.

"What the hell...?" Caley turned to look at Pat and gasped. The water gushing from the tap was bright red, and then it darkened a little and the consistency changed, became thicker. A coppery smell wafted up from the sink. "It's blood!" she cried, the colour of her face turning grey. Almost as soon as it had started, the colour changed back to normal. The girls glanced at each other then back at the now clear water. Pat moved the kettle toward the tap and this time was able to fill it. As she placed it on the stove and waited for it to boil, a sudden feeling of complete calm washed over her. She felt like she belonged in the house and needed to defend it. The sensation was strange but not unpleasant.

"I don't know about you, but whatever the weather is doing tomorrow, I think we should leave this place and find somewhere else. There are too many weird things happening around here for my liking." Caley's tone was solemn and tinged with fear.

"I agree some strange things have occurred, but we're tired, and by morning we might feel totally different. Let's wait and see what we think then, okay?"

"Are you *mad*? Why the hell would we feel totally different in the morning? Is the criteria us living through the night or something?" Caley retorted, her eyes wide, her tone incredulous. "The atmosphere in this cottage just isn't right. There's something almost... *evil* here. I can sense it."

The kettle had begun to boil, so Pat was making the tea and had her back to Caley. "I can understand you being a bit scared, but don't you think you're exaggerating a tad? I'm usually the one sensitive to all things paranormal, but apart from two unnatural occurrences, there's nothing here which gives me cause for concern."

"So what about the room neither of us wants to go in?"

"Ah, yes. I will concede there's paranormal activity in that room, and the atmosphere inside is not exactly... welcoming, but as for the rest of the house, I feel quite comfortable here." She turned to face Caley with two steaming cups of fruit tea in her hands and was confronted by a face filled with incredulity.

"Why are you suddenly on another planet to me? Everything we've seen and felt, everything that's happened has freaked you out as much as it has me, but now you're so laid back about it you're almost horizontal."

"Maybe I'm just able to put things in perspective easier than you. You're letting your fear blind you to what a lovely place this is and how ideal." She handed a cup to Caley who took it and shook her head as she turned away.

A loud banging noise interrupted their argument. Caley put her cup on the worktop, well away from the edge, and walked toward the noise. It was coming from the room they dared not enter. The door appeared to be shaking in its frame and was where the hammering came from. Having located the source, Caley immediately returned to the kitchen and began pulling out whatever metal pots and pans she could find and began loading them in front of the door. Several trips later, a barricade about two feet high sat there. She then returned to the kitchen one last time to grab her cup. To her surprise, half the contents had vanished.

"Pat? Have you been drinking my tea?"

"No, of course not. Why?"

"My cup was full and now it's half empty." Caley crossed her arms over her chest and glared suspiciously.

Pat moved across the room and picked up her cup. "The same thing's happened to mine. Look!" She held the cup out, and Caley glanced inside. The exact same amount was missing from Pat's.

"And you still think there's nothing wrong with this place?" Caley's voice was accusing.

"It's just spirits playing tricks on us. There's nothing to get worked up about – honestly. They mean us no harm," Pat replied with confidence.

Caley began to walk from the kitchen, and with a touch of hysteria in her voice said, "There's just no reasoning with you! I can't take this anymore. I don't care what the weather's like, I'm going, and if you've got any sense, you'll come with me."

The spell Pat was under continued to keep her calm and rational. "C'mon, Caley, it's getting dark out and you won't be able to see where you're going. You'll get lost. I swear to you, there's nothing to fear here. We'll be safe, and if you still want to go, we'll make tracks in the morning, okay?"

"Are you sure we'll be safe?"

"Positive."

Caley took a deep breath and let it out slowly. She really didn't want to leave alone, especially now it was dark. "All right, I'll stay, but I still don't like it."

Oh, no. They're really on the verge of waking the house up. I don't know how to stop them as I am. What can I do? He watched the lounge where Caley sat staring at the fire as she sipped her drink. *She's the sensible one*, he thought. *Her senses about the house are correct, but her friend, she's the one likely to set things in motion. If I show myself, they're likely to kill me. How can I stop this?* His fear was real. After all, he was living proof of what could happen. He continued to observe Caley from his hiding place.

A short while later, Pat appeared with two plates of steaming food in her hands and cutlery shoved in her pocket. She handed one to Caley, along with some cutlery, before sitting across the room from her friend. Caley looked at the food, wondering where

Pat had got some of the ingredients from. Deciding she didn't want to know, she thanked her friend and started to eat.

After dinner, Caley became extremely tired and couldn't seem to stop yawning. She felt her eyelids begin to droop and knew it was time for bed. In some ways she was glad to see the back of the day and fervently hoped tomorrow would be better. She said goodnight to Pat and, after brushing her teeth, climbed into bed. As soon as her head hit the pillow, she was asleep. Pat followed after a few minutes.

As soon as both girls were asleep, he emerged from his hiding place and became human once more. William set about cleaning the mess they'd made until it was spotless again. He then added another log to the fire and sat in his favourite chair. His two hundred years of the curse were almost up, and he was desperate to return to his human form for good, but if the girls didn't leave in the morning... the outcome would shatter him. His "clock" would restart from the beginning, and he couldn't bear the thought of another two hundred years in the disgusting form of a spider's body with his hands as legs.

An idea popped into his head. He rose and crept upstairs, and taking each of the girls' backpacks and the cooler bag, he placed them outside the front door. Walking into the drying room, he began to check how wet their clothes still were. As they were still too damp to wear, he pulled some off the line and draped them on the kitchen stove, turning them regularly. When the first set was dry, he swapped them with the rest and dried them in the same way. He'd just finished re-pegging the last of it when he heard the door to the office open, and a shiver of fear ran down his spine.

He heard the furniture in the lounge scraping along the floor as they were all moved at once and then a huge roar from the fire. Melezdra began to chant, calling forth spirits trapped in the walls and floor. The voices multiplied as more joined her. He walked to the kitchen and peeped around the door. The pentagram and symbols on the floor glowed red, and as each new spirit appeared in their corporeal form, they joined the high witch in a circle around it. Once they had all been summoned, he heard her say,

"My sisters, it is a full moon. We must enforce the curse on this house and summon the unholy one." She began to chant and everyone joined in.

William could feel the wall and floor moving beneath his hands and feet. He tiptoed back into the drying room and sat on the floor, head in his hands. He knew only too well what was coming next. There was a roar, and then a male voice could be heard booming off the walls. "Why have you summoned me, witch?"

"It is a full moon, oh great Abatu."

Before he had a chance to answer, there was a gasp from the top of the stairs. The noise had deliberately woken Pat, and she'd got up to investigate. Suddenly all eyes were on her, and she found she couldn't move or speak. Panic and fear seized her; she couldn't even cry out, which scared her even more.

"And who is this?" Abatu asked, licking his lips with his forked tongue and gazing at Pat lecherously.

"She goes by the name of Patricia, my Lord," the high witch answered.

"She will make a worthy companion for me until the next full moon, Melezdra. What a wonderful surprise." He beckoned Pat with a finger. "Come here, my dear. Let me take a closer look at you." Pat began floating down the stairs and found herself directly in front of the demon but just outside the pentacle. Clearly terrified, she stared at the monster. Abatu looked at her, then with one finger pointed at her pyjamas, they were ripped from her and left in a heap on the floor. He gazed at her naked, shivering form and smiled, showing his pointed, black teeth. "Oh yes, she will do very nicely." He freed her legs and made her step into the pentacle.

Abatu kissed Pat, forcing his lizard-like tongue down her throat while his hands caressed her. A quiet chanting began around them, which got louder as he forced himself upon her. Futilely she struggled against the pain, and with a roar, he finished then put her back on the ground. Pat clung to him, not from desire but because her legs felt so weak she didn't think they would hold her up.

The cadence changed, and although she had no idea what was being said, Pat realised the words had changed. Abatu enfolded her in his arms just as she realised there was something snaking up her legs. She looked down and saw tendrils sprouting from the floor, winding themselves around both of them and pulling them down.

Pat watched in horror as her feet disappeared into the wood and her legs began to follow. She tried to scream, but nothing came out; she tried to struggle and pull her feet out, but they were stuck fast. As the chanting reached fever pitch, Abatu and his unwilling victim were pulled faster into the floor until there was nothing left of them.

Melezdra had a satisfied smile on her lips. "Well, my friends, that went much better than we could have hoped. The appearance of the woman was an unforeseen bonus and has strengthened the curse on this house one-hundred fold. Our work is done until the next full moon, so it's time for us to retreat into the walls. Thank you all for your enduring commitment." She began to chant, and one by one her coven returned to spirit form and vanished into the walls. As her own body began to change, she walked across the room, into the office, and closed the door behind her just as the symbols around the pentacle stopped glowing.

William waited for several minutes before emerging from his hiding place and walking into the lounge. Pat's ripped pyjamas remained on the floor; he picked them up and deposited them outside on the veranda. He spent the next few minutes putting the furniture back before going into the kitchen and preparing a meal. Once he'd cleared it all away, he went upstairs and entered the room Pat had occupied. William snuggled under the covers and fell asleep.

When the first rays of dawn crept through the window, William awoke to find himself returned to the disgusting form he hated so much. He heard noises of stirring from the other room and scuttled into one of his hiding places.

Caley rose a few moments later and went into the bathroom. She washed, cleaned her teeth, and dressed in the clothes she'd worn the previous night. Noticing her pack was missing, she walked into Pat's room saying, "Wake up sleepyh..." Not only was Pat absent, all her things were too. She searched the house and in the drying room discovered only her clothes on the line. A shiver of apprehension ran down her spine. Caley walked to the front door, opened it, and located all the packs plus shredded pyjamas on the doorstep. She picked up the scraps of material and screamed.

After yelling Pat's name over and over, she collapsed to the ground sobbing. No one came to her aid.

She dashed into the house, grabbed her dry clothes and boots, and walked out of the cottage, slamming the door loudly behind her. Once she'd got her boots and coat on, Caley grabbed the packs and cooler bag and hurried away from the cottage without a backward glance.

Several days later, William awoke one morning to find himself in his human form. He danced around the bedroom laughing. He'd done it! Now he could enjoy the rest of his days in the home he'd loved for so long. *I'll find a way to drive out those witches and their demon, you mark my words!* he thought.

His next two days were heavenly. He was able to sit and read in the daylight, chop wood, gather berries, go hunting, and generally enjoy doing all the things he used to do before Melezdra cursed him.

The third morning, he awoke to find himself returned to the hideous form he'd endured for two-hundred years. He cried bitter tears as he realised the curse on his cottage applied to him too. He'd spent more than two nights sleeping there as a human and this was his punishment. In his mind he railed against the unfairness of it, of the witch turning his own home against him.

Several hours later, when he'd calmed down and accepted his fate, he became quite philosophical. As he looked down at his beloved lounge, he thought, O*h well, I'll know what to do next time!*

FOREVER
By Lee French

Mrs. Tucker urged her two boys down yet another dirt and gravel road in a frigid downpour, the burlap wraps on their feet offering no protection from the wet and mud. Tall dogwoods flanked the entrance to the Connors' smooth carriage drive. Shrubs guided the wide path to and around the forest-green two-story house. Raised beds covered with canvas tarps dominated the front yard, their herbs and vegetables already harvested and cleared. Hemlocks and beeches blocked the view of the next nearest houses in every direction.

The trio shuffled up the stone path to the wraparound porch, each carrying a burlap sack with all their belongings. Sheltered from the rain, the younger boy swiped a hand over his short black hair and flung water away. Mrs. Tucker sighed at her threadbare wool coat and soaked wraps, hoping the Connors wouldn't turn them away as the Baxters, Barneses, Laytons, Jaspers, and Bradys had. She couldn't do this and keep her job for long, and even with it, they'd run out of money for food in another week.

Exhausted from the walk, the older boy sat on the top step of the whitewashed wood deck and rubbed his face. He knew better than to complain out loud. His brother sat beside him and they leaned together.

Mrs. Tucker patted both boys on the head and turned to knock on the front door. It opened before she touched it. Mrs. Connor, a slim white woman with blonde hair swept up in a neat bun, looked the Tuckers over and raised a delicate eyebrow. Her broad-striped blue frock coat covered a crisp, white cotton dress. Mrs. Tucker yanked her hand back for fear of sullying the woman's fine clothes.

Not wanting to hear a sneer in the lady's voice, Mrs. Tucker launched into her story without waiting to be greeted. "Mrs. Connor, excuse me. I'm Mrs. James Tucker. I'm looking for live-in work. I been keeping the Baxter house for two years and they happy with me, but ain't got no space for me and my boys after

Mr. Tucker passed few days back. My boys ain't no trouble and they do a good job washing up in the kitchen. I can cook, clean, sew, and watch after littles."

Mrs. Connor's brow lifted in surprise, and she crossed herself. "I'm sorry for your loss." Her bright green eyes took in the boys slumped together, and she gave Mrs. Tucker a long, slow looking-over. Pity shaped her mouth into a sad smile, and she wondered if they'd have been better off as slaves. "You're in luck, Mrs. Tucker. Mrs. Baxter mentioned you were looking for work and said nice things about you. Mr. Connor can't pay much, but he can give you and your boys a roof, a bed, and meals."

Breaking into a relieved smile, Mrs. Tucker nodded. "Thank you, ma'am. We work hard, I promise."

Mrs. Connor's heeled boots clacked on the warm honey-wood floor as she led them inside. They passed through the mud room entry, where Mrs. Tucker and her boys peeled off their foot wraps and left them behind. It opened into a living room with a brown and green rug and matching couches and chairs around an oval coffee table. Shelves filled with books and curios took up most of the wall space, and heavy green curtains reached the floor beside the windows. Stairs led to the second floor on the left side. Through an empty doorway, Mrs. Tucker saw the big iron stove in the kitchen. Another room held a formal dining table and a filled china cabinet.

Two young girls sat in the living room, dolls in their hands and faces open with curiosity at the visitors.

"Millie, Tara, this is Mrs. Tucker and her two sons. They're going to stay with us and do the cooking and cleaning."

"Call me Lucy," Mrs. Tucker said with a deferential bob of her head. "This is John and Marcus."

Tara opened the window in her bedroom to the cooling summer evening and leaned out, thinking about climbing down. It seemed a long drop from the edge of the roof to the ground, but she wanted to try it in the daytime before trying to sneak out at night. Sticking her foot out, she gripped the windowsill and scraped her foot along the red oak shingles. One slid under her shoe, and she squeaked in fright as she slid.

Pulling herself back inside, she panted to catch her breath and resolved to ask Marcus to fix that shingle. Thinking of him sent her gaze down to the small cabin beyond the gardens he'd shared with his older brother for over three years now, since John's fourteenth birthday.

Both young men would be inside it now. As she watched, a figure emerged from the cabin. She saw John lift a hand to shade his eyes and peer toward the woods on the back edge of the property. He turned and jogged away, intent on collecting deadfall for firewood.

Eager to catch Marcus alone, Tara ran to the stairs. She straightened herself and took dainty, deliberate steps down. Millie sat in the living room, fussing with white ribbons. Their mother bent over the final, delicate stitches for Millie's wedding dress. Lucy hummed in the kitchen, busy making bread for dinner.

"Where are you going?" Mrs. Connor asked without looking up.

Tara stifled a sigh and flashed a bright smile. "Outside for some fresh air."

Mrs. Connor nodded, focused on her work. "Don't go far. I've got Miss Kelly coming to weave spells for the wedding tomorrow."

"Yes, Mother." Pleased she had no need to lie or sneak, Tara smiled and strolled out the front door in her garden clogs. She walked around the house in the warm sunshine, avoiding the windows so her mother wouldn't see her. Sheets hanging limp on the clothesline screened her from view out the back window. Tara peeked past the edge and watched Lucy until she moved out of sight. Seizing her one chance to go undetected, Tara darted across the stone path between the beans and squash to the cabin and wrenched the door open.

"Whuh?" Marcus sat on his cot, sewing a brown patch over the knee of a pair of wool pants. He looked up in the gloom of the windowless house and squinted to see Tara, breathless and gazing at him. He cracked a wide smile, though a thrill of fear ran through him. If anyone caught them together, he'd be strung up or worse.

"Your hair looks nice, Miss Tara."

She patted her head and beamed. "Thank you. Will John be back soon?"

"Probably." Marcus set the pants aside and stood, taking her in his strong arms. "I found a place in the woods we can go. I'll check to make sure no one is watching and you run that way." He pointed at the near back corner of the yard. "Wait out of sight. I'll find you."

Her belly fluttered, and she touched his face with delicate fingertips. His dark skin contrasted with hers so beautifully, and she loved the way he looked at her. No one else ever made her feel wanted in the same way. His kisses warmed her fingers and toes, and she longed to bare herself for him in every way.

Brushing a strand of hair from her face, he stared at her inviting lips. He inhaled her subtle perfume, noticing she'd dabbed her favorite rosewater on her neck for him. A door slamming shut in the distance reminded him of the danger he courted every moment they stayed. Pulling away, he grabbed the handle on the slat-wood door and yanked it open. "We need to go."

She fought to catch her breath and nodded. "Yes. We do."

Trying to seem casual, Marcus stepped outside and raised a hand to shield his eyes just as his brother had. "Go. Go now. No one is around or looking." He watched Tara rush around the back of the ramshackle house he and his brother had built from odds and ends of wood found in the forest.

He shut the door and noticed his mother waving from the back window of the main house. She smiled at him, and he returned it with a nod while he pulled his suspenders over his brown linen shirt and onto his shoulders. Anticipation made it hard for him to keep from running after Tara. He forced himself to breathe and walk.

John emerged from the trees, arms full of deadfall, before Marcus could escape his sight. "You done with them pants?"

"Nah." Marcus shrugged and groped for an excuse to get out of working for a while. "My leg cramped up from sitting like that. Gonna go walk it off. I'll take care of the stable after."

Dropping his load beside the bleached gray wall of their cabin, John rolled his eyes. "Just get it done before Mr. Connor gets home."

"I know," Marcus said. "I will."

John huffed his disbelief and walked away, shaking his head. His little brother would be the death of them if he couldn't pull his head out of the clouds. All that book learning Miss Tara helped him with would only bring trouble. Better to be proud of who he already was and do what he could with his God-given gifts.

Marcus ducked his head and shambled away with a fake limp. When he reached the tree line, he straightened and scanned for a cerulean dress. Tara waited for him a little farther in. He rushed to her side. Careful to constrain himself, he took only her small hand in his and tugged gently to pull her along through the forest. When she opened her mouth, he touched a finger to his lips to shush her. She wished he'd touched her lips instead but stayed quiet.

Following the path he'd marked with smeared red berries on the hemlocks, he led her deeper into the woods. He made sure she skirted around patches of mud and helped her climb over fallen tree trunks covered with moss and lichen. Finally, they reached a mound of ivy and mallow dotted with ruffled purple flowers and glowing in a shaft of sunlight.

Tara gasped in awe. Golden motes hovered around the flowers, tiny pinpricks of magic filling the glade with splendor. "How did you find this place?" she whispered, afraid to break whatever spell kept it so enchanting.

One side of Marcus's mouth quirked into a grin. "Wait. There's more." He led her down a carpet of springy clover and pushed an armful of vines aside to reveal a hollow. "It's hiding a room."

A soft glow suffused the inside with lavender light, and sweet honeysuckle wafted out. He lifted a foot to step inside the small room with leaves for a floor and stems for walls.

Worried they'd bring the wrath of whoever created such a wondrous shelter, Tara pulled on his arm, stopping him from entering. "Maybe we shouldn't wear boots inside."

Marcus looked down at the floor. He'd stepped inside when he first found it and saw no sign of damage from that earlier foray. Still, he had no qualms about playing along. Better, her concern gave him a wicked idea.

"Maybe...." He coughed and rubbed the back of his neck. When he'd pictured the moment in his head, it seemed more romantic than this. "Maybe we shouldn't, ah, wear *anything* inside."

Tara's eyes popped wide, and her pale cheeks flared crimson. Though she'd imagined taking her clothes off for him many times, it had always been at night in her bedroom. "I couldn't," she gasped. "Not in the open like this."

Rather than argue or wheedle, he cupped her chin and kissed her. It began tender and turned passionate. She forgot her inhibitions in his hands. When he fumbled with the buttons down the front of her brocade sacque, she pushed his hands aside and undid them herself. He pulled away long enough to tear his shirt off and toss it aside.

Without her coat, Tara found the air chill and pushed Marcus inside the shelter. They fell together on the bed of leaves, him cushioning her fall. She laughed as he kissed her neck, a bubbly sound to mark the shedding of carefully controlled restraint. Once he'd managed to pull her dress off, his struggles with her corset made her giggle until he freed her from it.

He stopped and gazed down at her bared skin for the first time, breathless at the sight. Brushing his hand down from her neck, he sighed. "I wish I could marry you."

She shivered and touched his face, the stubble on his chin tickling her fingers. Jealousy at Millie flared in her belly. Her man could touch her and hold her in the open. "I would say yes if you could ask."

Marcus took a deep breath and met her eyes. He imagined her in a fine gown like Millie's, waiting for him in a proper church. In front of the congregation and God, they declared their love and received blessings to bring children into the world. None of that could be theirs. Mr. Connor would skin him alive and all his friends would help. He and Tara could run off together, but it wouldn't matter. They'd never find a preacher willing to marry them no matter where they went, and even strangers would string him up for daring to love a white woman.

"A secret," he whispered. "It'd have to be a secret."

Still beneath him, Tara gulped. His body burned like fire against hers. She thought about all the flowers he'd picked for her, all the times he'd given up his coat for her, so many times when his kind words had chased away her tears, and how safe he always made her feel. No white man had ever made her feel half as beautiful or loved.

"Yes, a secret wedding."

Marcus's heart swelled. He wished Millie's wedding had already happened so he knew what to say. "Now?" When she nodded, he cast about for the right words. Though he wanted to invoke God, he worried the preachers would somehow find out. He took a deep breath and did his best.

"I call upon the spirits of this magical place to grant me my one wish. I pledge myself to you, Tara, in this life and the next. Though we can't show it outside, in here, I'm yours for all time. Do you pledge the same?"

Too nervous and pleased to smile, Tara gulped and nodded. "Yes, I do."

Much later, Marcus lay back with Tara draped across his body, stroking her hair and wishing this moment would never end. As their breathing slowed, he noticed it sounded different in a way he couldn't explain and craned his neck to look around. "Tara?"

"Hm?" Languid and satisfied in a way food had never managed to accomplish, Tara's eyes fluttered, and she shifted to snuggle closer.

"There's more room in here than before." Careful to keep her from sliding, he propped himself up on one elbow. The hollow now extended away from the front vine curtain, almost as big as the cabin he shared with John. Golden motes hovered near the ceiling, their glow revealing the ivy walls and a depression in the center covered with and ringed by silver-flecked granite stones. Four short cedar logs lay crossed atop it with twigs stuffed under and around them.

Tara raised her head and rubbed her eyes. When she opened them, wonder made her mouth fall open. "Magic," she breathed.

They stood together, with Marcus able to reach his full six feet of height under the roof. Hand-in-hand, they walked around the enchanted grotto house. "For us. It did this for us." Pulling Tara into his arms, he kissed the top of her head.

"Someone cares about us." Tara beamed up at him and wished they could stay here forever.

Gazing into her eyes, Marcus brushed a stray wisp of hair from her face. "This is God's work. We should honor it." His face fell as he thought about the world outside. "But I have to clean the stables before your father gets home or he'll whip me and John both."

"I'll get into trouble if I'm gone too long." Tara nodded and sighed. "We'll come back tomorrow. Maybe we can live here someday, but it'll have to wait at least until we set up something for water and food."

"We'll work something out." He kissed her as long as he dared before going to fetch their clothes.

"If you don't never go into town, you ain't never gonna find a girl to marry or a real job." John slung the old flour sack over his shoulder. Everything he owned fit inside. He'd never come back to this wretched little house again except to visit.

"I like it here well enough." Marcus shrugged and pushed the door open for his brother. "Besides, someone needs to look after Mama."

John snorted. "Mama can take care of herself, and Mrs. Connor is good to her. You gotta take care of you. Can't sit around pining after Miss Tara your whole life."

Marcus froze and tried to cover it with a cough. He looked away. "Don't know what you're talking about."

"Right. Like you ain't never thought about getting 'tween her sheets. I seen you watch her. She ain't never gonna be yours, and sooner you get that, sooner you find a girl you *can* have." John punched his brother in the arm as he walked out. Cool autumn air greeted him, the citrus musk of the neighbors' newly opened roses on the breeze. "All them books you read and your dumb head has to go and want for a white girl."

Thankful his face never betrayed a blush like Tara's, Marcus rubbed his arm. "I just think she's pretty. There's no harm in looking."

"'Til Mr. Connor notices. Then there's plenty of harm." John led them around the house to the street. Mama and his girl already waited for them at the black witch's shanty. "Watch yourself is all I'm saying."

Marcus glanced back at the house and saw Tara in the

window. She smiled at him. He cringed when John smacked him upside the head.

"Stop it." Grabbing his arm, John hauled him up the street. "I'll make sure you meet a bunch of girls today."

Marcus let himself be hustled away from Tara without complaining. He'd be back tonight, and they'd sneak off in the dark. Without John sharing the cottage, they didn't need to go all the way to their magic flower cabin anymore. They still would, because that place meant too much to abandon. Their first time had been amazing. Since then, he'd learned how to please her better. No other woman would ever be good enough.

Throughout John's simple wedding to a girl from town, Marcus thought about all the secret things he did to brighten Tara's cloudy days. So far, she liked it best when he snuck into her room through the window and left flowers on her pillow. She'd find them later and look out her window to smile and wave at him. Nothing short of having her in his arms filled him with so much joy.

Over the next few hours, he suffered through John introducing him to ten different girls his age, all unmarried and interested. Mama introduced him to a man in town willing to hire him as a bookkeeper and took the job for him. He'd start next week whether he wanted to or not. As the sun set, he walked Mama home, hunched against the chill.

"You gonna go meet one of them girls tomorrow?"

"No, Mama. I didn't like any of them."

Lucy put out an arm to stop her son and looked him over. For a few months now, he'd walked with his head higher, though it seemed like he kept looking over his shoulder. Half the time when she went looking for him, she couldn't find him, though he always got his work done. "You already got a girl."

He hung his head, not knowing how she knew and scared she'd guess right about Tara if she could see his face. "Yes, Mama."

She rolled her eyes and cuffed him. "Why you sneaking about and keeping her a secret? Bring her around and marry her. You got a job in town already. This ain't hard."

He shrugged and scuffed his boot in the dirt. "Her father doesn't like me."

"You take me over to her house tomorrow, and I'll tell him where to put his airs. Ain't no girl too good for my boy. You got book learning and clean up nice. Plenty of men'd be happy to have you as a son-in-law."

He shrugged again and didn't look her in the eye.

Lucy gripped her son's shoulders. Something had put fear and shame in his heart, though she could tell he felt powerfully strong for this girl, whoever she might be. "Marcus, you listen to me. I'm real proud of you. I was born a slave, so was your daddy. We never been schooled nor learned letters or nothing.

"You got chances and choices we never did. John, he never much cared for his letters and all that. He's gonna be a laborer like his daddy. You got something special. Don't settle for that bitty little shack in Mr. Connor's backyard. Make something with yourself. You hear me, boy?"

"Yes, Mama." He nodded and still stared at his worn boots. With his new job, he'd be able to get new boots and clothes. Money would help him take care of Tara too. "I'll talk to her. Maybe we can work it out ourselves."

"Good. You do that. And if that don't work, I'll take a swing at it." She wanted him to hold his head up and show fierce determination. When he didn't, she sighed and put her arm around his shoulders. "Don't wait too long, and make sure she's worth it."

The rest of the walk passed with Marcus mentally scrambling to figure out how to hold his mother off. She'd badger him until he either brought a girl to meet her or brought her to meet a girl's father. If she'd figured out he had a girl, he wouldn't be able to convince her they'd ended things unless Tara rejected him. The idea of that stung, and he hoped it never happened.

Tara watched the first snow of winter as it drifted down against the smoke roiling from Marcus's stovepipe chimney in the background. She wondered how they'd meet without their footprints giving them away. She could go to his cabin, but staying there for any length of time would be noticed, especially with his new schedule.

He left for work before breakfast, came home after supper, did his chores, and went to bed late. She hadn't seen even a glimpse of him in a week. His day off fell on Sundays, the same as her father's, making it hard to meet at all. She longed for his smile and his touch in their secret space.

"Tara, we're going to visit Millie for the day." Mrs. Connor offered Tara her cloak and muff.

"I don't want to go," Tara said. She shook her head to stifle the thrill she felt at the possibility of being left alone in the house. "It's too cold out."

"That's why you need your cloak and muff," Mr. Connor said as he adjusted his top hat in a mirror. "Besides, you've put on weight, so you should have an easier time handling it."

Mrs. Connor sniffed behind him. "She hasn't put on *that* much weight. But you should really get out and do things. Sitting around inside won't help anything. You need to meet young men so they can court you."

"I don't want to be courted." Tara knew she sounded whiny and didn't care.

"I see." Mr. Connor checked his brass pocket watch and harrumphed. "In that case, I'll just pick a husband for you and be done with it."

Mrs. Connor thumped his arm. "You'll do no such thing. Tara, you're listless because it's been cloudy for a week. Come out and get some fresh air. You'll perk right up."

Tara heaved a sigh she hoped sounded weary and put-upon. "I'll go outside, but I don't want to go anywhere."

Mrs. Connor's mouth went thin. If her daughter wanted to be an old maid, she could be an old maid. Millie, already pregnant, would make up for her. "Fine. But Lucy is coming with us so she can see John. You'll be here with only Marcus if you need anything, and he can't cook." She tossed Tara's cloak and muff onto the chair by the door, sniffed, and walked out.

After the door slammed, Mr. Connor jabbed a finger at Tara from across the room. "You'll be polite to whatever young man I bring home to meet you or you'll be flogged. If he chooses to court you, you'll marry him. Are we clear?"

Tara paled and nodded, frightened he might hit her. "Yes, Father."

167

"Good." He straightened his frock coat and nodded his satisfaction. "We'll be gone for a few hours."

She watched him stride out and jumped when he slammed the door. Though she wanted to run outside to get Marcus, she waited until she saw her father drive the carriage past the front windows. Throwing her cloak and muff on, she stepped into her garden clogs and hurried outside. These footprints made no difference; not only would the snow cover them, but her parents would assume she went out because she needed Marcus to help her with something.

At his cabin, she threw the door open and slipped inside to find it only marginally warmer than the outside. Already wearing his coat and boots, Marcus lurched to his feet and wrapped his arms around her. She slipped hers around his neck and kissed him. His chilled hands slid down her back to rest on her hips.

He pulled away, eyes heavy with weariness, and looked at her in the dim glow from the fire in his stove. Her loose hair fell across her chest and down her back in waves he wanted to touch. "This place is too dirty for you."

"Come to the house. It's warm there." She ran her hands through his hair, scraping her fingernails on his scalp.

"We'll get caught."

"The house is empty and will be for hours."

Her faint perfume sent his mind spinning. "We're not married there."

She grabbed his hand and pulled him out through the door. "It doesn't matter. We'll get lost in the snow, or we'll leave footprints to reveal our secret place. Please, Marcus."

Unable to resist her begging pout, he followed her to the house and held the door for her. They shed coats and shoes at the door. He tried to grab her, and she hopped out of the way. Laughing, she ran for the stairs. Though he knew how this would end, anticipation chased his fatigue away and he gave chase.

In her room, she stopped and attacked the buttons of her dress. He kicked the door shut and yanked his shirt off. Their hands flew through routines each knew well by now. Eager and blood pumping, he wrapped his arms around her from behind to trail kisses down her neck and shoulder.

"How could you forget something so blasted obvious as the day Millie and Andrew visit his parents?" Mr. Connor scowled and cracked the reins. The worst part of this fiasco of a trip had to be leaving Lucy behind for the rest of the day. It meant he'd have to eat his wife's cooking tonight, in addition to having to come out again later to pick her up. On a warm summer day, he'd leave her to get herself home, but he wasn't cruel. He wouldn't force an aging black woman to walk ten miles in the snow.

"I'm sorry I've ruined your day," Mrs. Connor snapped. "I thought it was tomorrow. Just get this infernal thing home already." She pulled the carriage blanket tighter around her legs, wishing her husband would spend the money for an enclosed one instead of this covered sleigh. Then Marcus would have to drive it, of course. Tara would have to come out because no one would be around to help her if she did anything stupid.

Mr. Connor harrumphed and pulled to make the horses turn up their street. "Do you think she's moved even an inch since we left?"

"Probably not."

"She's going to plump like a cow at this rate."

"Don't call your daughter a cow."

Mr. Connor ground his teeth together. "Do you know what's gotten into her lately? She seems unusually weary and lackluster lately. Over a month now, if I'm remembering right."

"She's sixteen." Mrs. Connor waved irritably. "Girls can get moody at that age, especially without a boy paying court. She probably thinks she's ugly or undesirable, or some other nonsense."

"We never had this trouble with Millie."

Mrs. Connor rolled her eyes. "Because all girls are the same. I expect she'll perk up if we can convince her to go out the next time the sky clears. Sunshine would do her a world of good."

The sleigh pulled into their drive, and Mr. Connor helped his wife out. He opened his mouth to call out for help with the horses then noticed the footprints in the snow. "I guess she decided to do something she needed Marcus's help with."

"She probably felt sorry for him all alone out there and brought him in for a reading lesson." Mrs. Connor folded her blanket. She huffed as her muff fell out of her coat pocket and rolled away. "Go get him. I'll be in shortly."

Mr. Connor grunted and stalked inside. He saw Marcus's boots and coat lying in a heap on the mud room floor and furrowed his brow. The boy usually hung up his coat when he came inside. Further, he saw Tara's damp clogs and cloak in another pile, and she definitely knew better. He continued inside, expecting to see them on the couch with slates and books, but the room sat empty.

He stomped the snow off his shoes and poked his head into the kitchen. When he saw nothing, he wondered what that girl could have gotten up to with that boy. Fell ideas pushed into his mind, and he hurried to the stairs. Halfway up, he heard Tara's voice and his heart stopped.

"Oh, Marcus!"

Mr. Connor ran up the rest of the stairs two at a time. He thundered down the hall and threw her door open to see his worst nightmare come true. His daughter, bare and beset from behind like a rutting animal, let out a ragged cry. Marcus's dark, evil hands gripped her perfect white hips as he defiled her. Stunned, Mr. Connor watched in silence, his mouth hanging open.

Eyes closed and oblivious in their ecstasy, neither noticed his abrupt entrance. Tara moaned.

Marcus groaned.

When Tara cried out with wordless pleasure, Mr. Connor shook himself and dove into the ghastly scene. He grabbed Marcus by the neck with both hands. "How dare you," he gasped. "I let you into my home!"

Marcus froze and opened his eyes. Terror surged through him. He could barely breathe around Mr. Connor's viselike grip.

Languid from her release, Tara rolled her head around. She registered her father and felt a wave of fear roil through her belly. Grabbing her quilt, she ducked behind the bed to wrap herself in it. "Father, no, please don't hurt him."

"Don't hurt him?" Mr. Connor roared. "After what he's done to you?"

Marcus grabbed Mr. Connor's wrist, praying he would let go and knowing he wouldn't.

Tara watched Marcus and saw the resignation as it closed his expression down. His face crushed her heart, and tears formed in her eyes. "He hasn't done anything to me, Father. Please let him go."

"Hasn't done--?" Mr. Connor glared at his little girl. "He's disgraced you!"

If only she hadn't brought him inside. They could have gone to their magical place instead. This was her fault. Tara sobbed as the weight of her choice crashed onto her shoulders. "I love him. Please let him go."

Mr. Connor stared at his little girl, not comprehending her words. "He's a pet, Tara. You don't bed your pets." Her insistence on teaching him to read had led to this. She'd come to see him as a man instead of a servant. "I'll deal with you later."

Tara watched through her hands as her father marched Marcus out backwards and threw him down the stairs. Her quilt wrapped around her body, she ran after them and reached the bottom of the stairs in time to see her father throwing Marcus out the front door. Hurrying to the front window, she stared out in horror as her father kicked Marcus in the gut.

With the sharp kick that sent him rolling off the porch and into the wood edge of a raised garden bed, Marcus knew his last hours would be filled with torture and agony. When he looked at the house, he saw Tara crying in the window with her hand pressed to the glass. She mouthed the words "I love you," and he lifted a hand to echo her.

"Don't you look at her," Mr. Connor snarled. He stepped between them and stomped.

Tara's anguish put fire in Marcus's belly. He lashed out with a fist, hitting Mr. Connor in the knee. The older man staggered and threw himself at Marcus. Both men punched and kicked at each other. Bigger and stronger, Marcus overpowered Mr. Connor. Straddling him with an arm raised to deliver a blow to the head, he hesitated when Mrs. Connor shrieked.

"Marcus," Tara wailed from the front door. "Run!"

Marcus lowered his fist, her command punching through his fog of rage. He looked down at what he'd done. Mr. Connor bled from his nose and mouth, with a tooth knocked loose and his eye already red and swollen. Other voices shouted nearby, coming closer.

Curling a fist in Mr. Connor's cloak, he ripped it away as he lurched to his feet and wrapped it around himself. "I'm sorry, Mr. Connor. Please don't punish my mama for what I've done."

Mr. Connor spat blood into the snow and curled up. Mrs. Connor rushed to kneel beside him. She pulled her own cloak off and draped it over her husband.

"If I were you," Mrs. Connor said, her voice quavering with too many emotions to think straight, "I'd run now and never look back."

Marcus gulped and saw people approaching, called by her screams. One man carried a revolver, another had a shotgun. A third had grabbed a thick, heavy stick. He looked to Tara and wanted to take her hand, but her mother was right. If he tried to bring her with him, they'd both be dead by nightfall. No matter what happened to him, she'd be safe so long as she stayed here. He blew her a kiss and fled up the road.

Tara watched him disappear into the snow. Two men with guns noticed and chased after him. One paused and fired his gun into the storm. She flinched at the horrific boom and stumbled inside. Another gunshot cracked in the distance. Panic sent her scrambling to her room. Throwing on clothes, she imagined her father cutting her off and throwing her out. She knew Marcus was all right. He'd circle around and make his way to their secret house. If she could bring enough supplies, they could live together in the woods.

Two men helped Mr. Connor stagger inside to a couch while another neighbor went for the doctor in town. Mrs. Connor bit back tears by force of will and hurried into the kitchen. They'd need hot water to tend to her husband. She couldn't spare any thought for her daughter now. Dealing with her would have to wait until later.

Upstairs, Tara grabbed a bag of everything she could carry and threw her window open. The bag went out first, tossed out to land in the snow on the ground. Sitting on the windowsill, she looked back at her room and everything she had to leave behind.

Mrs. Connor shouted her name, startling her into action. She backed out of the window, scraping her boot on the slick roof until it caught. Trusting the route she'd used many times before, she put her weight on her foot to climb out.

The wind whipped up, blowing snow in Marcus's face. He cringed inside the cloak, praying not to lose his way. Only one place would offer him shelter now. Trying to stay lucid, he shook his head and wondered at the miracle that kept any of the bullets fired from hitting him. Though it made no sense, he swore he'd seen a Colt revolver pointed at him. Had he heard a gunshot? Maybe. After that moment, he remembered nothing but snow and thought he must have ducked behind a tree by instinct.

His back and shoulder ached where he'd hit the raised beds, and his neck hurt from Mr. Connor choking him. Both feet had gone numb already from the cold, forcing him to stumble from tree to tree. One hand, its fingers painfully chilled, held the cloak shut in a death grip. His privates hurt too, though he didn't recall a blow landing there. Maybe he'd hurt himself in the scuffle with Mr. Connor without noticing until now.

Glancing behind him, he saw the snow swallowing up his tracks and sighed with relief. When he found the secret house, no one else would be able to track him to it. The next hemlock he lurched to had a smear of berries he recognized, giving him hope. Following the path he'd forged months ago, he watched for signs of Tara's passage and found none. The snow might have covered her tracks, or she might have decided to wait for the storm to pass.

Despite the cloud cover, a thick shaft of sunlight gleamed down onto the snow-free mound, and he staggered inside to collapse on the soft, spongy leaves. A fire crackled on the stones, filling the small house with warmth and the earthy smell of cedar. Beside it, a new iron pot hung from a spit he could move over the fire. Beyond it, he thought he saw a new water pump handle.

Tara slept beside the fire in a ruffled pink nightdress with a blue and white quilt covering her legs. Her golden hair gleamed in the firelight, and he longed to touch her. Crawling across the leaves, he noticed his body warming. Every inch of him hurt, though a cursory inspection revealed no injuries.

Dismissing the matter, he pressed his body in behind hers and wrapped an arm around her. She shifted and mumbled in her sleep. He kissed her neck. When that didn't wake her, he tucked his arm under her head and pulled her back to kiss her warm, inviting lips. Her eyes fluttered open, and she smiled at him.

"I thought you were dead," she murmured.

"Me too." He brushed the tip of his nose against hers.

"Bless this house for bringing you back to us." Tears of joy spilled down her cheeks.

He brushed her face to wipe the wetness away. "Us?"

Her smile widened, and she took his hand to place it on her abdomen. "I'm pregnant."

Though he thought he remembered only a bit of rounding, her belly now seemed swollen enough to hold a small melon. "That's wonderful. We can stay here forever."

"Forever." Tara sighed as he brushed his lips against hers then trailed a line of kisses down her neck. "In this life and the next."

unique electronic & print books

ABOUT THE AUTHORS
(in no particular order)

Alison DeLuca is the author of several steampunk and urban fantasy books. She was born in Arizona and has also lived in Pennsylvania, Illinois, Mexico, Ireland, and Spain. Currently she wrestles words and laundry in New Jersey.

Carlie M A Cullen was born in London. She grew up in Hertfordshire where she first discovered her love of books and writing. She has been an administrator and marketer all her working life and was also a professional teacher of Ballroom and Latin American dancing until 2013 when she had to stop due to health reasons.

Shaun Allan is the creator of many prize winning short stories and poems. A writer of multiple genres, including horror, humour and children's fiction, Shaun goes where the Muse takes him – even if that is kicking and screaming. Shaun lives with his one partner, two daughters, three cats and four fish! Oh, and a dog.

Connie J. Jasperson lives and writes in Olympia, Washington. A vegan, she and her husband share five children, eleven grandchildren and a love of good food and great music. Music and food dominate her waking moments and when not writing or blogging she can be found with her Kindle, reading avidly.

Ross M. Kitson is a published author in the fantasy genre, with an ongoing series (The Prism Series), a number of short stories on Quantum Muse web-zine and several stories in Steampunk and fantasy anthologies. Ross works as a doctor in the UK specializing in critical care and anaesthesia. His love of speculative fiction and comics began at a young age and shows no signs of fading.

Marilyn Rucker has been writing catchy tunes with bizarre lyrics about off the wall situations since she was a zygote. She's had success placing songs in situation comedies ("I Love Your Smell" in the King of Queens) and independent zombie movies ("A Zombie Human Love" in Z, A Zombie Musical) She's big in Finland and Germany and with Xena fans (for "If I Could Be Like Xena"). Her novels are also quirky and off the wall, and will hopefully also be big in Finland.

Stephen Swartz grew up in Kansas City where he was an avid reader of science-fiction and quickly began emulating his favorite authors. He studied music in college and, like many writers, worked at a wide range of jobs: from French fry guy to soldier, to IRS clerk to TV station writer, before heading to Japan for several years of teaching English. Now Stephen is a Professor of English at a university in Oklahoma, where he teaches many kinds of writing. He still can be found obsessively writing his latest manuscript, usually late at night. He has only robot cats.

Lisa Zhang Wharton was born and raised in Beijing, China. She is a graduate of Peking University and University of Minnesota. She is an engineer by education and an author by avocation. She has previously published several short stories about life in China in various literary magazines. Her short story "My Uncle" has won a second prize in a WICE sponsored Paris Writer's Workshop. "Last Kiss in Tiananmen Square" is her first full-length novel. She lives in St. Paul, Minnesota with her husband and son.

Lee French lives in Olympia, WA with two kids, two bicycles, and too much stuff. She is an avid gamer and active member of the Myth-Weavers online RPG community, where she is known for her fondness for Angry Ninja Squirrels of Doom. In addition to spending much time there, she also trains year-round for the one-week of glorious madness that is RAGBRAI, has a nice flower garden with one dragon and absolutely no lawn gnomes, and tries in vain every year to grow vegetables that don't get devoured by neighborhood wildlife.

Irene Roth Luvaul lives and writes in Washington State. Born and raised in Texas, she wrangled lawyers for many years, until she and her husband moved to a Pacific Northwest mountaintop to raise sheep. An editor for Myrddin Publishing Group and lover of all things adventurous, Irene writes historical fiction and multi-genre short stories.

MYRDDIN PUBLISHING GROUP BOOK LIST

WWW.MYRDDINPUBLISHING.COM

URBAN FANTASY ~ PARANORMAL ~ ROMANCE

GIRLS CAN'T BE KNIGHTS by Lee French (New Adult)
Everyone knows girls can't be knights.

YUM by Nicole Antonia Carson (YA)
Can Jim and his great-granddaughter Emily stop the carnage?

Brawn Stroker's Dragula: The Journal of Dee Flaytable by Nicole Antonia Carro (Mature Readers)
When the Vampire Queens battle, who will win? Dragula is pure smut. Enjoy!

HEART SEARCH SERIES by Carlie M.A. Cullen (New Adult)
HEART SEARCH, book one: Lost, HEART SEARCH, book two: Found
One bite starts it all. . .Fate toys with mortals and immortals alike, as two hearts torn apart by darkness face ordeals which test them to their limits.

THE GUARDIAN SERIES by Joan Hazel (New Adult)
Book I THE LAST GUARDIAN, Book II BURDENS OF A SAINT
Delta Pack is an elite force of shape-shifters charged with maintaining order in both the shifter and human communities. High adventure and sizzling romance!

HIRED BY A DEMON by Gypsy Madden (YA)
A simple babysitting position goes terribly awry for Vara…Urban fantasy at its best!

~~~

SCIENCE FICTION

LAND OF NOD SERIES by Gary Hoover (Appropriate for all ages)

Book I—The Artifact,
Book II - The Prophet
Book III – The Child

Jeff Browning has been haunted by terrifying dreams since the mysterious disappearance of his father (a renowned physicist). But when he finds a portal in his father's office, he must overcome his fears in an attempt to find him.

THE DREAM LAND Series By Stephen Swartz, under Tangential Books

Book I Long Distance Voyager,
The Dream Land 2 - Dreams of Futures Past,
The Dream Land 3 - Diaspora

An epic of interdimensional intrigue, alien romance, and world domination by a couple of high school nerds mashed with psychological thriller and time travel.

MAZE BESET TRILOGY by Lee French (Superhero science fiction)

Dragons In Pieces
Dragons In Chains
Dragons In Flight
Superheroes in denim.

~~~

STEAMPUNK

THE CROWN PHOENIX SERIES by Alison DeLuca (Teen)
The Night Watchman Express

Devil's Kitchen
The Lamplighter's Special
The South Sea Bubble
A magic typewriter, time-travel, a mysterious train—high
adventure written with Edwardian flair!

The Infinity Bridge (The Nu-Knights) by Ross M. Kitson (Teen)
Three teenagers are propelled into an action-packed race against
time, involving alternate realities, airships, clockwork killers.... and
Merlin.

~~~

LITERARY FICTION
AFTER ILIUM by Stephen Swartz (Mature readers)
Seduction and betrayal on the road to Ilium. An epic of
interdimensional intrigue, alien romance, and world domination by
a couple of high school nerds mashed with psychological thriller
and time travel.

AIKO by Stephen Swartz
AIKO, a love story wrapped around a mystery, is a modern version
of the Madame Butterfly story.

TALES FROM THE DREAMTIME by Connie J. Jasperson
(Literary Fantasy, Mature Readers)
Three grownup Tales from the Dreamtime in one novella....A
conversation with Galahad, a prince on a quest and a goddess in
mourning, a stolen kingdom and the Fractal Mirror. Three tales of
wonder and great deeds, three tales of heroes and villains.

LAST KISS IN TIANANMEN SQUARE by Lisa Zhang
Wharton
A coming-of age story set against the historic and devastating era
in Chinese history. With the cultural significance and family bonds

of "The Kite Runner", this book explores the way in which one's past is never forgotten.

MY "UNCLE" (Mothers, Daughters, and Affairs, book 1) by Lisa Zhang Wharton
Twenty years old Meihua had always been in love with her mother's former lover "Uncle" Weiming. Now she is on a search for him.

~~~

EPIC FANTASY

TOWER OF BONES SERIES by Connie J. Jasperson (Epic Fantasy) under BARD Books
Book I, Tower of Bones
Book II Forbidden Road
The Gods are at war, and Neveyah is the battleground.

MOUNTAINS OF THE MOON by Connie J. Jasperson (Epic Fantasy) under BARD Books
Wynn and his companions face a gauntlet of jagged peaks and deadly traps. Danger, mystery, and dark prophecy—who will fall and who will survive?

HUW THE BARD by Connie J. Jasperson (Medieval Fantasy, Mature Readers)
Fleeing a burning city, everything he ever loved in ashes behind him, penniless and hunted, no place is safe. Abandoned and alone, Huw the Bard must somehow survive.

DAMSEL IN DISTRESS by Lee French under Tangled Sky Press (Dark fantasy)

Even cut flowers can bloom.

AL KABAR by Lee French (Epic Fantasy)
The Fires blaze in dozens of wild, capricious Dancers. The Waters anoint only one champion, one Al-Kabar to serve--and save--the people of the desert.

OF ICE AND AIR by Carlie M.A. Cullen (Dark Fantasy)
Kailani faces isolation, wild beasts, rogue soldiers, and more as she battles to return to the Ice Palace. With the stakes so high, can she make it back alive?

PRISM SERIES by Ross M. Kitson (Epic Fantasy, Mature Readers)
Darkness Rising 1 – Chained
Darkness Rising 2 – Quest
Darkness Rising 3 – Secrets
Darkness Rising 4 – Loss
Darkness Rising 5 - Broken
Bravery is measured in moments. The forces of darkness are rising—and tragedy awaits even the most heroic.

THE GREATEST SIN SERIES by Lee French and Erik Kort under Tangled Sky Press (Epic fantasy)
    The Fallen
    Harbinger
    Moon Shades
Prophecy. Secrets. Lies. It's all an illusion.

SIN by Shaun Allan (Dark Fantasy) under Singularity Books
What would you do? Could you kill a killer? Does the death of one appease the deaths of a hundred? What about that hundred against a thousand? What if you had no choice?

DARK PLACES Series by Shaun Allan (Dark Fantasy)

DARK PLACES
DARKER PLACES
Dark Places. Thirteen stories. Thirteen poems. Thirteen doorways.

SUFFER THE LITTLE CHILDREN by Shaun Allan (Dark Fantasy) under Singularity Books
Specially commissioned by Universal for the release of the movie sequel 'Sinister 2', Suffer the Little Children is "genuinely terrifying!"

MR. COMPOSURE (The Purge: Anarchy) by Shaun Allan (Dark Fantasy) under Singularity Books
Specially commissioned by NBC Universal for the release of the film The Purge: Anarchy, Mr. Composure is "simply superb" and ranked #1!